To Dar'...

A
KABBALISTIC
UNIVERSE

By the same author

Adam and the Kabbalistic Tree
Kabbalah and Exodus
A Kabbalistic Universe
Psychology and Kabbalah
School of the Soul (School of Kabbalah)
Tree of Life: Introduction to the Cabala
The Way of Kabbalah
The Work of the Kabbalist

A
KABBALISTIC
UNIVERSE

Z'ev ben Shimon Halevi

SAMUEL WEISER, INC.

York Beach, Maine

First American edition published in 1977 by
Samuel Weiser, Inc.
Box 612
York Beach, Maine 03910-0612

99
11 10 9 8 7 6

Library of Congress Catalog Card Number: 88-50809

ISBN 0-87728-349-4
BJ

Cover illustration is "The Universe," a miniature from the manu-
script *Scivias* by Hildegarde of Bingen, c. 1150. Reproduced
here by kind permission of Otto Muller Verlag, Salzburg, Aus-
tria.

Printed in the United States of America

The paper used in this publication meets the minimum requirements of the American National Standard for Permanence of
Paper for Printed Library Materials Z39.48-1984.

to my Teachers

Contents

Plates

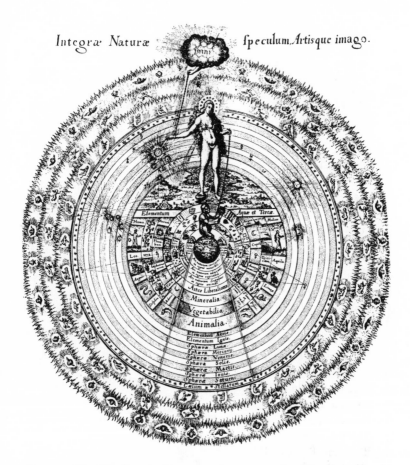

Figure 1. The World. *In this seventeenth-century version of Jacob's Ladder, the Tetragrammaton hovers on the edge of Manifest Existence. Within the first World of Emanation the Divine hand holds the chain of Will, which extends down through the Worlds of Creation and Formation to the Bride or Malkhut of the World of Asiyyah. She in turn imparts the influx through stellar, planetary, elementary and organic realms to the monkey-mind of natural man, who seeks to comprehend the Universe by the senses.*

Preface

Each one of us at some point in our existence has looked up at the Milky Way and sensed the vastness of the Universe. Some have perceived that beyond the furthest galaxies lies another dimension, an unseen order that contains and governs our world. In every generation a few penetrate this cosmic veil and view Creation from its Source. Their vision is handed down to us through Kabbalah so that we, as Jacob, might also behold the great ladder between Earth and Heaven with its descending and ascending Hosts of God.

London, Spring 5735

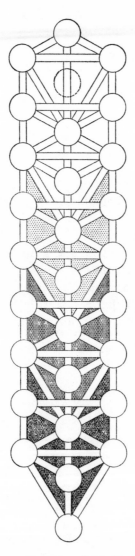

Figure 2. Jacob's Ladder. *Containing all Manifest Existence, this basic Kabbalistic diagram sets out every level within the four interpenetrating Worlds that emanate from the first Sefirotic Tree of Azilut. Known as Jacob's Ladder, it defines the down-flowing paths of Creation and the up-rising ways of Evolution towards its source as the great cosmic cycles go out from Divinity, reach their extreme in matter and return for completion in perfection.*

Introduction

'God's place is the World, but the World is not God's place.' In this Kabbalistic saying is the clear statement that while God is present in Existence, God is quite separate from it. This mystery of Immanence and Transcendence is where God and the World meet in intimate and mutual knowledge. Such a miracle forms the basis of the Kabbalistic view of the Universe.

In early times Kabbalah was divided into two parts, the Work of the Chariot and the Work of Creation. The former, whose subject is man, is concerned with human nature* and the methods of penetration into the deepest and highest level of man's interior universe.† The latter is the study of the exterior cosmos of the four Worlds, their origins, construction and function in relation to man and God. This is the subject of this book.

Operating between the pillars of revelation and Tradition, Kabbalists studying the Universe based their work on the Bible and the instruction of their spiritual mentors. From this union of written and oral lines came, if the Kabbalist merited it, a direct cognition of what Existence has been, is and shall be until the End of Days.

Of the oral connection little can be said, because the imparting of knowledge is contingent upon the subtle relationship between teacher and student. Of the written tradition there is much to be seen, for every age has produced its version of the Changeless Teaching. These accounts by past Kabbalists, however, are often

---

*See author's *Adam and the Kabbalistic Tree* (Bath, England: Gateway Books; York Beach, ME: Samuel Weiser, 1974).

† See author's *The Way of Kabbalah* (Bath, England: Gateway Books; York Beach, ME: Samuel Weiser, 1976).

difficult to read not only because they speak of Worlds out of natural sight, but because they were cast in the language of their particular school and period. Thus the allegories of early apocalypses and the metaphysics of the medieval era are almost unintelligible to people in the present, unless they have the key to the Kabbalistic scheme.

The key is, as it has always been, the Sefirotic Tree. This diagram of all things Called Forth, Created, Formed and Made is the objective image of the Manifest Universe at every level. With its aid, the present outline is my attempt to portray a general picture of the World based on ancient and modern findings. Its language is of our time and its depth is the limit of my comprehension of what I have been taught of Kabbalah.

Man's place is the World. As the image of God, man has the greatest possibility of realizing the Immanence present in the Universe. The World provides the conditions for man's work towards perfection, and in return man aids the World towards its completion, so that that which has been separated reunites. In this mutual knowledge, the Immanent and the Transcendent meet in the place of God.

וייקץ יעקב משנתו ויאמר אבן יש ידוה במקים הזה
ואנכי לא ידעתי: וייךא ויאמר מה־נורא המקום הזה
אין זה כי אם־בית אלהים וזה שער השמים:

And Jacob
awaked out of his sleep, and he said:

'Surely the LORD is in this place; and I knew it not.'
And he was afraid, and said: 'How full of awe is this
place! this is none other than the house of God, and this
is the gate of heaven.'

GENESIS 28

Figure 3. Ezekiel's Vision.   *Below, captive in the natural world of Babylon, the prophet perceives the upper three Worlds in the vision of a Chariot, Throne and Man. This symbolic diagram of the four levels of Manifest Existence was used by early Kabbalists to study and express the qualities of the non-sensual Universe. Like all Kabbalist formulations, Ezekiel's description is but an allegorical image of another reality and should not be taken literally.*

1. Symbol and Reality

How is the indescribable described? It is impossible, and yet mystics of all traditions have attempted it despite the fact that they will fail and create only a faint after-image of something direct experience alone can give. Why then do they try? It is because natural man would have no conscious idea of the supernatural Worlds if he were not shown that there is an order and purpose even within the invisible realms. To be without knowledge, no matter how dim, is to be in utter darkness dominated by fear and confusion. Every natural man knows this from the experience of arriving in a place he does not know at the dead of night. Indeed this is natural man's condition when he intrudes into the next World during or after life.

Mystics down the ages, and Kabbalists are no exception, have continually tried to describe the Worlds beyond the natural senses. Sometimes they have used myth, and sometimes elaborate metaphysics. All the devices used have intentionally fallen short, because they are merely representations of reality. Occasionally they have succeeded, but for the wrong reasons, when people without comprehension have taken the symbolism for the real thing. This is why in the course of time new analogies have had to be constructed so as to free people from an image that comes to bar rather than bridge the view between the natural and supernatural.

The oldest formulation of the upper worlds in Kabbalah is that of the Bible. In its first chapters, the Creation of the Universe is set out in a myth that contains a very precise account of the unfolding process from the Eternal to the natural world. The Talmud or the rabbinical commentaries on the Bible contain references to the underlying cosmology, but there is no complete scheme, and what mention is made is often cast in oblique allegory. The post-Biblical classic, the *Sefer Yezirah*, or Book of Formation, sets out its world picture in terms of astrology blended with scripture, number, alphabet, anatomy and geography. Its imagery is complex and peculiar to its time. This same situation occurs with the *Sefer HaZohar*, or Book of Splendour, whose vast texts range from the most sophisticated metaphysics to simple folk belief. The latter-day Kabbalists of the immediate post-medieval period extracted what they could from these previous formulations and developed their own version of the Worlds above and their workings. Isaac Luria is the most widely known Kabbalist of this epoch, and his main ideas are still with us today, although much modified by the eighteenth- and nineteenth-century Kabbalists of Eastern Europe.

The present work is based on the pre-Lurianic view. It is less intricate than Luria's scheme, but more verifiable in theory and practice: this truth can be tested easily in relation to the body and the psyche,* because they are more perceivable phenomena than the subject of this work. Here again we pose the question, 'How does one describe the indescribable?'

The answer is that all that is to follow is a synthesis of images, an amalgam of Kabbalistic presentations of what the Universe is, how it works and what its purpose is. Nothing that is said is any more than a symbol for a reality that the natural mind cannot ever comprehend. If however there is a shift, a lift in the perception of the reader, then the image may dissolve to reveal that reality.

---

*See author's *Adam and the Kabbalistic Tree* (Bath, England: Gateway Books; York Beach, ME: Samuel Weiser, 1974).

GOD

אַתָּה הוּא עַד שֶׁלֹא נִבְרָא הָעוֹלָם· אַתָּה הוּא מִשֶּׁנִּבְרָא
הָעוֹלָם· אַתָּה הוּא בָּעוֹלָם הַזֶּה·· וְאַתָּה הוּא לְעוֹלָם הַבָּא·

Thou wast the same before the world was created; thou
hast been the same since the world hath been created;
thou art the same in this world, and thou wilt be the
same in the world to come.

MORNING SERVICE

2. Before the Beginning

God the Transcendent is called in Kabbalah AYIN. AYIN means No-Thing. AYIN is beyond Existence, separate from any-thing. AYIN is Absolute Nothing.

AYIN is not above or below. Neither is AYIN still or in motion. There is nowhere where AYIN is, for AYIN is not.

AYIN is soundless, but neither is it silence. Nor is AYIN a void – and yet out of the zero of AYIN's no-thingness comes the one of EN SOF.

EN SOF in Hebrew means the Endless. As the One to the Zero of AYIN, EN SOF is the Absolute All to AYIN's Absolute Nothing.

God the Transcendent is AYIN and God the Immanent is EN SOF. Both Nothing and All are the same.

Beyond the titles of AYIN and EN SOF no attributes are given to the Absolute. God is God and there is nothing to compare with God.

Tradition states that God willed to see God and so God's Will, symbolized by light, shone nowhere and everywhere. Thus the EN SOF AUR, the Endless Light of Will, was omniscient throughout Absolute All. From God knowing All, God willed the first separation so that God might behold God. This, we are told, was accomplished by a contraction in Absolute All, so as to make a place wherein the mirror of Existence might manifest.

The place that was vacated was finite in that it was limited in relation to the Absolute All that held it. This act of contraction, or *Zimzum*, as it was called, brought about the void of Unmanifest Existence even though it was, we are told, the size of a dimensionless dot in the midst of the Absolute.

Unmanifest Existence is the place of Emptiness. It is quite different from No-thingness because it is a thing, although it is a negative, like the void in a hollow ball. Such a condition must exist so that Positive Existence may come into being within it.

According to some Kabbalists, the Will of God that surrounded the vacated space in the symbol of the EN SOF AUR began to penetrate as a beam of light into the void of Unmanifest Existence. This brought into focus the three factors that made the void. The first was the Will of the Absolute, the second the Act of allowing it to happen and the third the Restriction to limit and contain the event. These three principles at work within EN SOF AUR are called by some Kabbalists the three Zahzahot or the three Hidden Splendours.

The Zahzahot were the hidden roots of what eventually would become the first of several sets of major laws that would govern Existence. They generated the processes of expansion and contraction overlooked by Will. Kabbalists sometimes regard them as the original acts of Mercy and Severity operating under the direct eye of the Absolute. While these Hidden Splendours lay outside both Unmanifest and Manifest Existence, they profoundly affected the nature of the Universe, which was the result of their interaction, as it came into being out of the Will of EN SOF.

The event of becoming occurred when the EN SOF AUR began to penetrate the periphery of the void. In the first penetration of the Kav, or light beam of Will, through the frontier between EN SOF and the void came the separation of Existence from the Absolute, because in the generation of positive Existence the EN SOF was concealed, hidden beneath the manifestation. Thus EN SOF is sometimes called the Concealed of the Concealed.

The first manifestation at the circumference of the void was named the Prime Crown. It has many other titles, like the Concealer of the Concealed, the White Head and the Crown of all Crowns. Most Kabbalists knew it by the God Name of EHYEH or I AM, where the Absolute allowed Existence to be.

The first Light, or first Sefirah, as this manifestation of Divinity is called, is the seed of all that was, is and shall be. It is the Light from which all other Lights, or Sefirot, emanate. At the margin between the Absolute and the relative Universe, it contains all the World in equilibrium. Until the Will of EN SOF AUR penetrates into the void and emanates manifestation, the Prime Crown is the unrealized possibility of all things.

When God willed the World to come into being, the seed took root and grew downward into the trunk, branch and fruit of a Divine Tree that would act as an intermediary between the World and God.

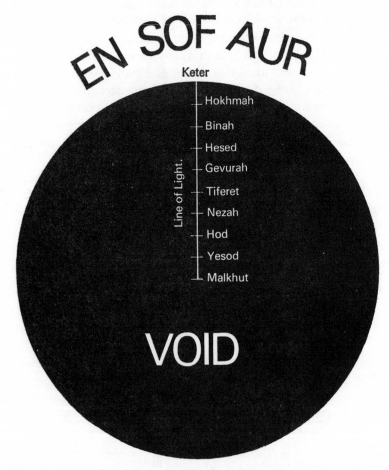

EN SOF AUR

Keter

Hokhmah

Binah

Hesed

Gevurah

Tiferet

Nezah

Hod

Yesod

Malkhut

Line of Light.

VOID

Figure 4. Line of Light. *In the midst of the all-pervading* EN SOF AUR *a space was vacated by the Absolute so that a positive manifestation could come into its negative existence. Into this void the Will of God, seen by some Kabbalists as a Line of Light, penetrated. Thus the Divine World of Azilut, whose root word means 'to stand near' was called forth.*

3. Manifestation

When God willed that the Line of Light should penetrate beyond the First Crown of Manifestation and proceed towards the centre of the Void, the interaction of the three Zahzahot brought about a second process. This was the law generated by a progression from the point of departure from the Absolute in the act of separation to reach the point of full manifestation, that is, the stages between the seed and the full-grown tree bearing the fruit seed for the next generation.

The phased progression comes about because the three Zahzahot exert their hidden influence on the flow of Light in the following manner. The First Crown is in a state of perfect equilibrium. But with the impulse to emanate coming from the Will of God it comes under the Zahzah, or Splendour of Action, and so becomes an expansive principle of power. This active aspect, however, is and must be checked by the Restrictive Splendour or it will over-extend the emerging Universe.

When the prime trio of Emanation had been established, the Line of Light then proceeded to repeat the process, with the Will allowing the next expansion and contraction phases to be completed in a series of three, until just before the end of the progression the Will resolved the Line of Light at the centre of the Void into what could be called the fully manifested synthesis of all that had gone on before. The Line of Light, on reaching the centre of the Void, is now seen as a series of Sefirot, or Lights, some being active, some being passive, with others at crucial points of equilibrium being the manifestation of the Will of God as it is emanated into Existence.

Some Kabbalists see the Line of Sefirot also as vessels, with each lower Sefirah receiving the emanating Will from an upper and imparting it to the one below. Here begins the complex study of metaphysics in which Kabbalists have sought to understand the nature and workings of what has come to be regarded as the Divine World of Emanation within the void of Unmanifest Existence.

The most well known of the metaphysical formulations of the Line of Light progression is the Sefirotic Tree of Life. This is more complete than, say, the formulation of the Lights and Vessels scheme, in which one is placed inside the other like a sequence of enclosing kernels and shells. The Sefirotic Tree contains all the laws that govern the Manifest Universe, in that it is based on the interaction of the three Zahzahot and the stages of Sefirotic progression from its inception into Existence to its resolution and return to the source of EN SOF.

The law of initiation, progression and resolution is called by some Kabbalists the Great Octave, because it is seen very clearly in the analogue of the musical major scale. In this, the upper Do is the First Crown, with the second note as the active and the third as the passive note. After Do Re Mi comes the interval of a semitone, which is crossed by the Will directly intervening to aid the impulse across to the next active note or phase of Fa. The octave then proceeds to Sol, a note of passive form. The flow is again helped by an act of Will which carries the emanation on to the active La and the passive Ti. At this point comes the last interval or semitone which is filled by the Will just before the impulse resolves in the last Do. Such a progression can be seen in the linear arrangement of the Line of Light, but it is most usually formulated into the diagram of the Sefirotic Tree.

The reason why the Tree is as it is, is because it demonstrates very graphically how the two prime laws of the triad and the octave combine to compose the Divine but relative World of Emanation. In this interaction the Do of the First Crown is the point of equilibrium and so acts as the fulcrum of Will to the scheme, while the notes of Re and Mi take up the active and passive roles to right and left of the middle point. This trio makes up what is called the supernal triad that heads the three pillars

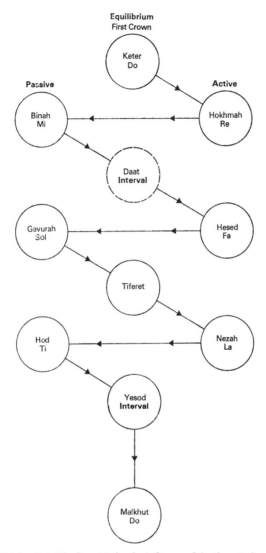

Figure 5. Lightning Flash.   *Under the influence of the three Zahzahot, or Hidden Lights, within the Godhead, the Line of Light and its ten-stage progression ordered itself into an octave arrangement of an initial Do, two alternating active and passive states and a final Do, with two crucial interval points on the central column as the Light came into equilibrium. This Divine pattern became the basis of everything that was to come into Existence.*

which are to be developed out of the influence of the three Zahzahot and the progression of Emanation. The first interval or semitone is placed just below the Crown. However, it is not regarded as a true note, for reasons that will become apparent later, but nevertheless it acts as the transformer between the supernals and the next pair of Fa and Sol. These Sefirot are situated in line with the two side Sefirot above and make the midpoints in the outer functional pillars that are emerging. The central Sefirah has again no obvious role except that it is the receptacle of all that has been and will pass on what will be. Here again the Will operates, although it performs as a non-note. The two last notes take up their place on the Force and Form columns, so completing the third pair of functional Sefirot. They in turn make two small triads, one with the central Sefirah above and one with the Sefirah of the semitone that fills the interval below. They also make a great triad with the lowest Do. The scheme of the Tree completes itself with the connecting of various Sefirot according to the law of sub-triads so as to reveal all the levels and functions within the perfect World that has been emanated from the First Crown.*

The ten Sefirot, plus the one non-Sefirah, are known by Hebrew names, based on Biblical roots, which describe the attributes of God when manifested in the Divine World. Words denoting the Sefirot collectively vary according to different Kabbalistic schools. For example, in one period they were called the Crowns, in another the Faces of God, and in another the Powers. There are many others. As for the particular names of the Sefirot, there is general agreement, with several exceptions. These are not so much differences as emphases in interpretation, because no name is anywhere near adequate to describe the Divine principle embodied in a Sefirah. The Hebrew names and their English equivalents are given in figure 6. There are several English translations for the same Hebrew root. This book uses a particular set because they are considered to be the closest to the function of each Sefirah.

Each Sefirotic name describes the quality of the Sefirah, although this is by no means apparent at first sight. Thus, for ex-

*See author's *Tree of Life* (London, England: Rider & Company; York Beach, ME: Samuel Weiser, 1975).

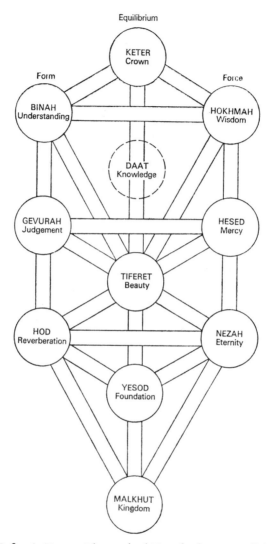

Figure 6. Sefirotic Tree. *The completed Tree of Life, as it is called, contains all the Laws that govern the Manifest Universe. Seen here in its medieval form, its Hebrew names and their English translations are only faint approximations of the Divine Attributes they are based upon. The Kabbalah has many versions of this diagram, ranging from the seven-branched candlestick of Moses to the complex sub-Tree system of Lurianic Kabbalah.*

ample, all the Sefirot on the passive pillar are receptive and have the qualities of Form, in that Understanding is the formulation of ideas, Judgement is exercised in response to something, and Reverberation is the echo to an impulse coming from any one of the other Sefirot. It is the same with the active pillar. Here the impact of revelation is seen in Wisdom, while the power that must be behind Mercy is enormous. Eternity is the principle of repetition, the incessant input necessary to make the world go round. The central pillar is concerned with Will and with the Grace which descends from the Crown through Knowledge to Beauty, which is the Sefirah that reflects the top to the bottom of the Tree. Foundation and Kingdom are respectively the manifestation of an image plan and the actualization of it in the Divine material.

The Sefirot are joined by twenty-two paths, which form a network of triangular sub-systems or triads. This arrangement is one of the several lesser laws that govern the relative Worlds. Their function is to enable the Line of Emanation to circulate generally as against just down the Lightning Flash, as it is called, of the Octave. By this system of paths, various minor combinations of flow can occur and so bring about different emphasis in specific parts of the Tree.

At this point in Existence, the Sefirotic Tree is the unchanging model of perfection. Within its field nothing is born, grows, decays or dies. It is the eternal paradigm of Law, the place where Divinity is manifest, where the Will of the Absolute may work upon the as yet uncreated Universe to come. As the attributes of the Divine set out in Existence, it is the mirror of the Image of God.

4. Divinity

The perfect and unchanging World that emanates from the First
Crown is eternal. While what lies beyond the First Crown is
timeless, the World of Emanation is time-full. Here is Existence
without end, as long as the Absolute wills it. Should God reverse
God's will to see God, the Universe would vanish and the void of
Unmanifest Existence be filled and dissolved into All and No-
thingness again. The World is sustained by the Will and Grace
of God. Until God ends Time the Emanated Tree of the Sefirot
will exist for ever.

Tradition calls the World of Emanation the World of Unity.
This is because while there is a system of relativity between the
manifest Divine Attributes, they are in fact expressions of the One.
From Keter, the Crown, all that *is* flows out, and in this emanation no thing is in isolation, for nothing can exist on its own. Only
God can be separated and transcendent, and so while the differentiation between Force and Form, between above and below, and
between one Sefirah and another, is precise, by their very relationship they all merge into a Unity of Divinity.

Keter, the Crown, is the manifest source of the World. As the
first manifestation it stands next to the Absolute but is separate
from it. The Hebrew name for Emanation is Azilut, whose root
also means 'to stand near'. This is a very precise description of a
place or World that is both outside and inside Absolute All and
Absolute Nothing.

The World of Azilut is the World of Divine Lights. It is also
called the Glory of God, which permeates the lower Worlds of
Existence as an unseen radiance. This impression of the Light of

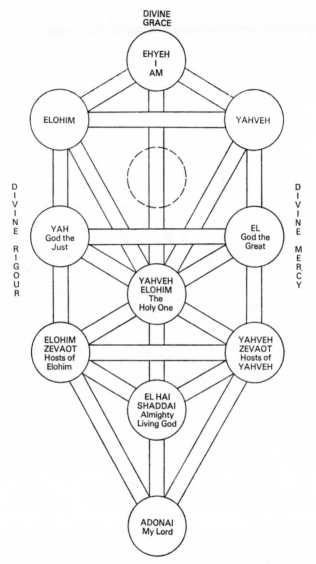

DIVINE
GRACE

EHYEH
I
AM

ELOHIM

YAHVEH

DIVINE
RIGOUR

DIVINE
MERCY

YAH
God the
Just

EL
God the
Great

YAHVEH
ELOHIM
The
Holy One

ELOHIM
ZEVAOT
Hosts of
Elohim

YAHVEH
ZEVAOT
Hosts of
YAHVEH

EL HAI
SHADDAI
Almighty
Living God

ADONAI
My Lord

Figure 7. Divine Names.   *In this scheme, the Names of God are arranged according to the qualities of upper and lower Divine Mercy and Severity, with the Presence of God manifesting at different levels on the central column of Will. Again, there are alternative versions according to Kabbalistic school. This is due to varying application of God's Biblical Names. In Sefirotic essence there is no difference.*

Manifest Divinity recurs in all esoteric traditions and comes down to natural men even in folklore. Among Kabbalists Azilut is described in many ways.

According to one formulation, God brought Azilut into being by ten utterances. These Ten Words came out of the Black Fire of Unmanifest Existence into the White Fire of Azilut. The Sayings, we are told, became the various aspects of Divinity in the archetypal plan of the Sefirotic Tree, and they are the Names by which God is called. Their arrangement developed as follows:

Out of Keter, the God Name of EHYEH or I AM, emanated the Will to be in Existence. Realized in the Divine title YAHVEH, whose root means 'to become', the second God Name is associated with Hokhmah or Wisdom, the Sefirah which heads the active column of force. The third God Name, associated with Binah at the head of the passive column of Form, is ELOHIM, whose literal translation is 'many Gods'. In Kabbalistic terms that is 'I will be manifested in many.' This triumvirate of EHYEH – YAHVEH – ELOHIM constitutes the Three Great Heads of Existence. As such they represent the Divine Mind and the World, and the Wisdom and Understanding of God, whose Ways are not our ways, whose Thoughts are not as our thoughts.

The God Names for Hesed and Gevurah, like the Sefirotic titles themselves, differ among the Kabbalistic schools. All titles, however, reflect the Mercy and Severity of Divinity.

In this book's scheme, the God Names of EL and YAH are used. The former, meaning simply 'God', is on the active pillar; the latter is a shortened version of YAHVEH. These two Names are lesser manifestations of the upper side of Sefirot. As such they indicate a significant and crucial mirroring in the small triad they both help to compose with Tiferet at the centre of the Tree: when joined together, they unite in the Combined God Name of YAHEL or YAHOEL, which is one of several titles given to the Azilutic Tiferet. The same occurs when the other combined God Name of YAHVEH-ELOHIM is also seen to be attributed to the key Sefirah of Tiferet. Here, at the place of Adornment, as Tiferet is sometimes called, is the confluence of the upper Azilutic World. Some Kabbalists call Tiferet the 'HOLY ONE – Blessed be He'.

The two lower functional Sefirot are known by the God Names of YAHVEH ZEVAOT and ELOHIM ZEVAOT, which being translated mean the HOSTS of YAHVEH and the HOSTS of ELOHIM. These multiple titles describe the executive operations of the columns of Force and Form. They carry out the directives of Divine Mercy and Judgement, and the plans of the Intellect of Divinity. As the HOSTS of God they implement, through repetition and reverberation, all the things that are willed to be done.

EL HAI SHADDAI, the God Name of Yesod, the Foundation of the Divine World of Azilut, is translated as the LIVING ALMIGHTY GOD. Here on the central column of equilibrium the Will of God is manifested in the image of Divinity. As such this title represents the appearance of Divinity, the Living Power and Glory to be glimpsed by those creatures that attain the highest levels of spirituality.

The last God Name ADONAI means MY LORD and is the title of the bottom Sefirah of Malkhut, the Kingdom. Tradition states that this is the place of the Shekhinah, the Presence of the Lord. It is the God of those creatures that cannot reach the upper parts of Heaven. As Malkhut is the Divine Presence, so the Shekhinah has its place, at Malkhut, in all the lower Worlds as the representative of the Immanence of God even in the densest of materialities.

While the God Names emanate from I AM in a Sefirotic progression, there is, however, a secondary series of Divine Names down the central axis of the Azilutic Tree: HE for Keter, THOU for Tiferet and I for Malkhut. These epithets indicate that the Absolute's Will has direct access to the World called forth in the Ten Divine utterances. It will be noted that there is no God Name for the Daat or Knowledge of the Azilutic Tree. This non-Sefirah is the Abyss between the three great Heads of the supernal triad and the rest of manifestation. To penetrate beyond this veil of the Holy of Holies is to see the Face of God before passing out of Manifest Existence.

Another Kabbalistic version of the World of Azilut is the figure of Adam Kadmon, the Primordial Man. This analogue is taken from Ezekiel's vision on the bank of the River Cheber, where the prophet saw the appearance of a vast man seated upon a likeness of a throne, which was carried by the appearance of a chariot drawn by four strange living creatures. Surrounded by a fiery brightness, the figure, in Ezekiel 1, is likened to the Glory of God. This human but divine model has been seen by some Kabbalists as the first perfect manifestation of the Absolute, as God the Transcendent sees God the Immanent in the image of Azilut.

The Divine Image of the perfect man occurs throughout Kabbalistic tradition. In its literature, perhaps the most well known but often widely misunderstood presentation is set out in a curious book called the *Shiur Komah*, which translated reads 'The Dimension of the Stature of God'. Such remarks in it as 'that the soles of his feet cover the Universe' are misleading to the literal-minded who cannot see that it means that the bottom plane, or Malkhut, of Emanation overlays the lower Worlds of Creation, Formation and Making. The book, full of number and name combinations, has inevitably been denounced by those who cannot see beyond the limits of the natural World. Even Maimonides, the greatest of learned rabbis, could not accept that the giant image was an allegory of something outside his Aristotelian philosophy and religious orthodoxy. Declaring that the book should be burnt, he revealed his limit of comprehension.

For those who perceive the inner meaning of Adam Kadmon's figure, it contains a wealth of knowledge concerning the World of Divinity. Generation after generation of Kabbalists examined and developed the theme of the Primordial Man, until in medieval Spain there was released into the public domain a detailed anthropomorphic diagram of the Azilutic World. This human scheme was presented in the Zohar, in the Books of Concealed Mystery and Greater and Lesser Assemblies, where the description of a vast head and the symmetry of its beard outlines an intricate and complex metaphysical scheme. In our example, we will set out the simplest version of Adam Kadmon.

The figure of Adam Kadmon is usually presented from the rear, out of respect for the verses, Exodus 33:20-3, which state that no man may see God's Face and live. However, Moses is allowed to view the back part of Divinity. The next thing that is noted about this image of the primal man is that the left side is dark and the right is light. This indicates not only the Form and Force aspects of Azilut but the Male and Female elements present in Adam Kadmon, because the figure is androgynous or an amalgam of the two sexes. The theme of sexual polarity constantly occurs in Kabbalah, as it is the most obvious symbol for the active and passive sides of any World, its inhabitants or events that occur under the Laws represented in Adam Kadmon. While in Azilut the two sides are embodied in one being, in later and lower Worlds the difference becomes more pronounced, until in the natural World of Asiyyah the active and passive columns are actually physically separated into the sexual division within and between plants, animals and people. However, at the level of Azilut, the Perfect World, the two sides are said to be in face-to-face union and like one being.

The next thing to be observed about the figure is that the three Sefirotic columns are clearly set out along the vertical axis of the body. The active Sefirot are on the right and the passive on the left, with the Sefirot of Will located on the median line running from the Crown down through the spine to the feet. In some Kabbalistic schemes the left and right are reversed like a mirrored reflection, so that the active appears on the left. This is merely because the image of Adam Kadmon has been visualized as facing us. Such differing standpoints sometimes cause some confusion among those who see diagrams literally and perceive no further than the logical explanation. However, the image is clear, if the principle is seen that, for instance, Hokhmah is always the active Intellect of Wisdom by its position by or on the head of Adam Kadmon, and that Hesed is always the active arm of the Divine man. Some Kabbalists place Hesed over the right breast, saying it is the positive side of the Divine Heart; the difference is insignificant, when the arm is seen to act in accordance with that side of the heart. Binah and Gevurah represent the left, passive or severe side of the head and heart of Divinity. Together, both side pairs of functional Sefirot are subject to Keter, which hovers as a crown over the head of the Divine man. The non-Sefirah of Daat or Knowledge is placed by some Kabbalists over the throat and mouth. Here, it is said, is the place of the Bat Kol, or Divine

Voice. The actual phrase means 'Daughter of the Voice', and it is
the Voice of the Holy Spirit, which is said to reside in this non-
Sefirah. A Biblical example of the Bat Kol is seen in the unearthly
Voice that announced the death of Moses to the Israelite camps in
Sinai. It is also to be found in more private circumstances in the
still small inner voice, and in the symbolic image of a descending
dove.

The central Sefirah of Tiferet is usually placed just below the
heart in the body, although some Kabbalists regard it as the whole
torso, which acts as the pivot for all the limbs and head. This concept is borne out in the Tiferet of the Sefirotic Tree. No doubt
there was the same idea of a nexus, in that the human solar plexus
with its radiating nervous system is an excellent symbol for
Tiferet. This central placing again emphasizes the division between
the upper and lower half of the World. While the intellect may
think, and the heart act through the arms, nothing can be accomplished unless the lower parts move the being into full action and
generation of events and offspring.

The idea of generation and creation is located in Yesod, which
is placed over the genitals. From here, Adam Kadmon can produce
another being or World, in his own image, except that it will be
at yet one more remove from the Absolute than he is. This newly
created being, in turn, can produce a next generation, but this is
yet another World distant from the Source of All. Yesod, as the
foundation of Adam Kadmon, is his organ of generation; as such
it carries the image of Adam Kadmon, but in seed both male and
female. In the Divine state of Azilut as such there is as yet no
fructification, no reproduction because there is still no lower
World of Creation to be inhabited by creatures. Yesod in Adam
Kadmon has to reside in eternal perfection until God the CREATOR
wills the next World into being.

On either side of Yesod, sometimes on the hips and sometimes
on the legs, are placed the Sefirot of Nezah and Hod. These
functional principles are called the supports of the Divine Adam.
As right and left legs, they implement the Grace descending from
above and transmit, with Yesod, the Will to the feet at Malkhut.
Here is where the being of Adam Kadmon touches the Created

Universe, when it comes into existence. As the lower half of the Divine body, all the Sefirot beneath the heart are seated in and are part of the Throne of Heaven, which is a Kabbalistic symbol for the Beriatic World of Creation that emerges out of the World of Emanation. This event occurs because of four distinct levels found in Azilut, which prefigure and eventually precipitate three further separate Worlds outside Eternity.

THE WORLD

ליהוה הארץ ומלואה תבל וישבי בה:

The earth is the Lord's, and the fulness thereof; the world
and they that dwell therein.

PSALM 24

5. *Separation*

In the image of the World of Azilut as a natural Tree, the root is Keter, with the trunk growing downward into branch and fruit. Like all Kabbalistic allegories, this contains a precise meaning and body of knowledge. First, it will be noted that there are four distinct levels, each performing a function at different points to the whole. The root acts as the drawer of *sustenance* from the Source of EN SOF, while the trunk creates the massive main *growth* and support of the Tree. The branches spread in all directions and take up the characteristic shape of the Tree, with the leaves constantly undergoing a change of *form* in the round of seasons. The *fruit* is the result of the other three levels and is bitter or sweet, strong or weak, fertile or barren according to the conditions and workings within the Tree. The fruit, moreover, is the seed of the next Tree, so that in its fructification it repeats the cycle and grows out of nothing into something immense and, in relation to its one ephemeral moment of conception, into an almost eternal being exactly like the tree that generated it.

The allegory of the reversed tree with its four levels and great cycle is one of many about the Azilutic World used by Kabbalists. The division into four levels stems from the text of Isaiah 43:7, in which it is said 'Even everyone that is called by my Name: for I have created him for my glory, I have formed him; yea, I have made him.' These four stages of manifestation are one of the secondary great laws of the World of Azilut and constitute a further division in the law of progression out of the interaction of the supernal triad of Keter-Hokhmah-Binah. In some esoteric traditions these four levels are seen as Fire, Air, Water and Earth;

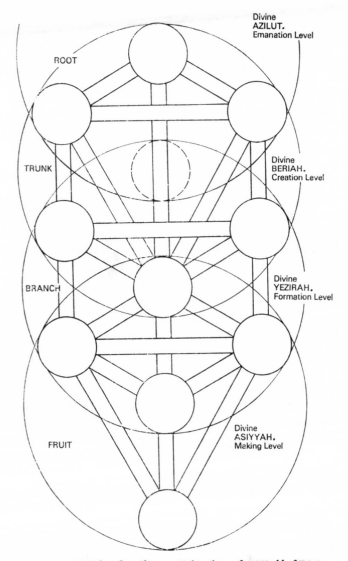

ROOT

TRUNK

BRANCH

FRUIT

Divine
AZILUT.
Emanation Level

Divine
BERIAH.
Creation Level

Divine
YEZIRAH.
Formation Level

Divine
ASIYYAH.
Making Level

Figure 8. Four Levels of Azilut. *Within the perfect World of Divine Emanation are four levels. Originating in the descending stages of the Lightning Flash, they are sometimes seen as the four aspects of an inverted Tree growing out of the Will of the Absolute. These four Divine phases generate the three separated lower Worlds of Creation, Formation and Making out of Azilut.*

that is, the four states of manifestation ranging from radiant energy through the gaseous and liquid conditions to the solidity of matter. In Kabbalah there are several variations on this elemental scheme, and these depend upon which way one is viewing the World. One example is that Fire and Water constitute the right and left pillars, with Air as the upper and Earth as the lower part of the central column of equilibrium. The most common scheme is that the Sefirotic Tree is divided vertically into four spheres of influence, with Fire or the Glory of the Lord (Ezekiel 1:27) as the Azilutic level of the World of Emanation, sometimes seen as the supernal triad and sometimes as a circle pivoted on Keter extending round through Hokhmah-Daat-Binah. Here again, different Kabbalists use slightly different models. This once more points to the fact that no analogue is exactly right. Only the Absolute can claim perfection. The rest is merely an approximation of a realm that cannot be defined in natural terms.

The rest of Azilut is divided, according to the quotation from Isaiah, into three stages, progressively removed from the Divine level of Emanation. They are the trunk or Created level, the branches or the Formed level, and the fruit or Made level of Azilut. As such they represent four phases of resolution in the Great Octave Emanation down the Line of Light or Lightning Flash. In the Tree of Azilut they are as eternal as any other law in that World but with a difference, because by their very differentiation they project the downward progression beyond the changeless World of Azilut to indeed Create, Form and Make quite new Worlds that fulfil God's Will to see God. Thus the Worlds of Separation, as they are called, begin from the World of Unity.

According to tradition the Azilutic World of the Sefirot acts as the interchange between EN SOF and the lower Worlds. In this way God, we are told, can view God as a man observes his reflection in a mirror. As the mirror is the intermediary vehicle, revealing, but in reverse, the image, so the World of Azilut is the opposite to God, who is the Reality to the mirrored likeness of the World. There the allegory, like all allegories, has its limitations, because Azilut is only the Divine instrument which creates everything that is called forth.

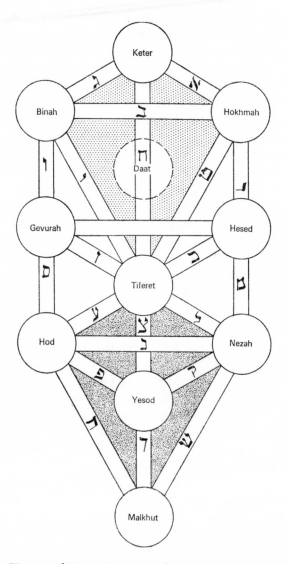

Figure 9. Upper and Lower Faces. *In this particular version, the shaded areas represent the upper merciful Face and the lower severe Face of the Tree. As mirror to the upper configuration, the lower Face is always subjective. Besides the crucial intermediary triad of Hesed–Tiferet–Gevurah, the Hebrew Alef-bet is shown. These twenty-two letter flow-paths join the ten Sefirot and complete Manifest Existence.*

The Sefirotic Tree, as it was first publicly formalized, probably in medieval Spain, is composed of ten Sefirot plus one non-Sefirah, twenty-two paths, sixteen triads and the four sub-divisions we have just discussed. There is, however, yet another major division that is to be noted, and this is the Sefirotic configuration of the upper and lower Faces. Now the term Face is frequently used in Kabbalah, but it does not always have the same significance to different Kabbalistic schools. To some Kabbalists it means just the Sefirot, to others exclusively Keter and Tiferet, while others relate the term to particular constellations of Sefirot like the group of Hesed, Gevurah, Nezah, Hod and Yesod that focus upon Tiferet. Those of the Lurianic school have a whole complex of Faces that appertain to individual Sefirot. In this work, I apply a specific sense whose rationale will explain how the upper and lower Worlds interlink.

The expressions Long and Short Face are used in the Zohar. These are not very explanatory translations of the Mercy and Severity of God. Some Kabbalists read them as just Keter and Tiferet in a vertical manifestation of Active and Passive on the Sefirotic Tree. Others, and I belong to this school, see the Long and Short Faces as the twin kite-like configurations shown in plate 9. In this, the image of the upper Face is reflected in the lower; moreover, while the upper Face is the imparter, the recipient lower Face becomes more complex, having new paths and triads. This is quite in order, because it describes the increasing complexity of laws and materiality as the level is removed further from EN SOF. Thus it is that the lower Face is more severe, that is, under greater law or Judgement, which is a crucial fact in the subsequent processes of Creation, Formation and Making.

Creation begins not, as many Western students of Kabbalah believe, in the Malkhut but in Daat and Tiferet of Azilut. Remember first our basic theory of Emanation: the supernal triad is the Azilut of Azilut or the Holy of Holies. From here the Lightning Flash crosses the interval of Daat, under God's Will, to begin to expand in Hesed. At Daat, Creation is called forth; that is, out of pure Emanation the Azilutic Creation (Beriah) is willed and comes into being. In Azilut, Hesed represents the principle of eternal

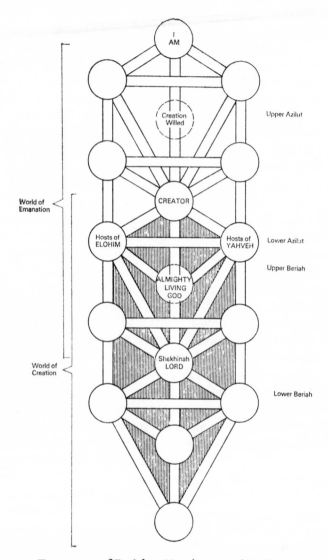

Upper Azilut

World of
Emanation

Lower Azilut

Upper Beriah

World of
Creation

Lower Beriah

Labels within the diagram:
I AM
Creation Willed
CREATOR
Hosts of ELOHIM
Hosts of YAHVEH
ALMIGHTY LIVING GOD
Shekhinah LORD

Figure 10. Emergence of Beriah. *Here the separated World of Creation emerges from the Tiferet of Emanation. Thus God the Creator and the Divine Hosts of Mercy and Judgement bring out of the lower Face of Azilut the upper Face of Beriah. Underlying the Daat and Tiferet of Creation resides the Divine* LIVING ALMIGHTY *and the Shekhinah or the Presence of the* LORD.

expansion and Gevurah that of eternal contraction, and so the essence of Creation, which is to create something out of nothing, is followed, as the impulse emerges from the Abyss of Azilutic Daat into the expansion characteristic of Creation and the constraint that controls and contains that Creation before it stabilizes in the equilibrium of Tiferet. Here at the centre of the Tree, the creative Force and Form are synthesized and begin fully to be. At this junction point of Tiferet, the essence of the level of Azilutic Formation occurs, and so Creation is actually given a recognizable form as it moves from the upper into the lower Face of the Tree of Azilut.

In terms of the God Names, or the Divine Attributes, the Azilutic level of EHYEH or the I AM of ultimate equilibrium, the YAHVEH of the active and the ELOHIM of the passive sides of Divinity bring about, through the Will of Divine Knowledge and the EL and YAH attributes, God the CREATOR, who is the YAHVEH-ELOHIM and YAHEL of the Azilutic Tiferet. God the CREATOR thus heads the lower Face of the Tree of Emanation, and so from this central focus there begins to emerge, out of the Beriatic or creative level of Azilut, a quite new and separate World of Creation.

As the upper Face imparts Grace to the lower Face, so the Hosts of YAHVEH and ELOHIM implement the Will of I AM and God the CREATOR, that is the Keter of Azilut and the Keter of Beriah, the now emerging World of Creation. As the flow of Emanation has already provided the base of a Face, so the lower Sefirot of Azilut create the upper Face of Beriah. There is, however, one major difference, and that is that the paths flowing into Yesod do not exist in the emerging upper Face of Beriah, because, like the Azilutic upper Face, it has the non-Sefirah of Daat, which coincides exactly with the Azilutic Yesod but in a lower and separate World. This coincidence of the Foundation of the upper World with the Knowledge of the lower is vital in the chain of Worlds that is to become known as Jacob's Ladder.

The emergence of Creation out of Emanation is implemented by the lower Face of Azilut. Here the HOSTS OF GOD (Nezah and Hod) and the CREATOR (Tiferet) form a creative Knowledge out

of the image of Divinity in the Azilutic Yesod. In this place of EL
HAI SHADDAI, the ALMIGHTY LIVING GOD creates and forms, in
Azilutic terms, the World he is to make at the Azilutic Malkhut,
which is to become the Tiferet of the World of Creation and later
the Keter of the World of Formation. Thus it is that Creation
begins in the Beriatic level of Azilut and overlays the Eternal
World of light with the first separated substance. Here the analogue of Creation acting as a shell around the kernel of Divine
Glory is seen, so that the Absolute is yet again concealed behind a
veil and separated beyond the intermediary World of the Azilutic
Sefirot from the Creation. Here also Time begins, as Creation
moves away from the Eternal and Changeless Perfection of Azilut
into the expansion and contraction that are the essence of the
Beriatic World of Creation.

6. Imperfection

Creation comes forth from the Divine and Unchanging World of Emanation. With it Time begins. Kabbalah, like many other esoteric traditions, sees this change from the Eternal into the Temporal as a vast impulse of cosmic movement. It all begins, however, with the Ten Sayings or Utterances with which God brought the World into Existence. Now in Hebrew the word *davar* means both 'to speak' and 'thing' or 'affair' or 'matter'. In Aramaic, the sister tongue to Hebrew and the language of much of the Talmud, the same word means 'to depart', 'pass away' and 'death'. All these meanings from the root *davar* indicate that out of the Calling Forth of Azilut the Worlds of separation, of retreat (another translation) from perfection, were initiated.

This situation is taken up by the Kabbalistic myth that the first efforts of the CREATOR were not quite what was wanted. Like an artist (who is a human image of the CREATOR), God's initial attempts were experiments. We are told that indeed there were several World's created and dissolved before our particular Universe was arrived at. Kabbalists explain these earlier Worlds as being faulty because they were not completed in the perfect image of Azilut; that is, while the upper Face of Beriah might be sound because it coincided with the lower Face of Azilut, the lower Face of Creation was, by definition, imperfect and unstable and therefore subject to distortion either because there was too much Force or too much Form. Thus one embryo Universe was excessively expansive and therefore diffused itself, and another was too contractive and liable to implode the Cosmos into an unviable rigidity. Kabbalists put this in a moral allegory by saying that God observed that an over-merciful Universe would make no check on evil while an extremely severe Creation would be unbearable for the creatures that would inhabit it.

The first hint that there are to be inhabitants comes in the clear differentiation between the titles 'World of Unity' for Azilut and the 'World of Separate Intelligence' for Beriah. The first Worlds and their denizens were named by Kabbalists as the Primeval Kings or the Malkhei Edom, the Kings of Edom who reigned before there were Kings in Israel. Now Israel is the Kabbalistic name for the World of Creation. This realm of Beriah is also called the World of the Throne, it being the seat of Ezekiel's Divine Man. However, before the first stable cosmos could come to be, the Matkela, or Balance of Scales, as the Zohar calls it, of the pillars of Force and Form and the upper and lower Faces of Beriah had to be brought into relative equilibrium. The term 'relative' is used because there were and still are, we are taught, pressures that cause considerable fluctuation within the Tree of Creation.

The primary influence comes from above, in that as Emanation comes into being, so its flow exerts an influx down into Beriah. This stems from the Will of EN SOF and the tension of differences between the Void, the perfection of Azilut and the imperfection of Beriah. Such a phenomenon is seen in the Natural World in the situation between the potential and actual or between high and low densities and pressures. The Azilutic tension, for obvious reasons, is considered beneficial, but there are others that are evil; that is what 'evil' ever is.

It is said that everything comes from God. Nothing can emanate from anywhere else. There is God, and nothing else exists unless God brings it into being. Therefore even evil originates from God. So we must conclude that if God is good then even evil must be a form of good, even though at a particular time and place it may appear as anti-God. It cannot be otherwise, or there must be an independent Evil Absolute whose essence, being chaos, could not create an ordered Universe, let alone maintain it and balance and bestow Grace. Evil begins with separation; that is, Evil begins with Creation.

As Existence moved from the state of Azilutic perfection in its projection and progression out of the four levels in Azilut, it took up the created state of several kingdoms of Edom. When these unbalanced monarchies proved to be too harsh or excessively lax, they were destroyed. However, the Forces and Forms that had composed them were not dissolved into nothing again, but remained present to the extreme left and right of the stable and satisfactory Tree of Creation that was eventually arrived at by the CREATOR's work. The Edomic Forces and Forms were, moreover, without a central axis of Will in their Trees, because it had been removed by the CREATOR, and so they were almost totally functional and mechanical, with only a dim consciousness in the intelligences who inhabited their excessively turbulent or rigid domains. These impure intelligences, which came to be called Arch-demons, were constantly to assault the realm of Creation, test its stability, and continually tempt the pure spirits that inhabited Heaven.

When balance had eventually been obtained in Creation, the creative Lightning Flash was allowed to reach the Beriatic Malkhut and there establish the Malkhut haShamayim, the Kingdom of Heaven, so beloved by that great Kabbalist Joshua ben Miriam of Nazareth. With this extension of the Line of Light in Beriatic reality complete, the first Cosmic Cycle began its impulse to unfold the Universe.

In Kabbalah, the great Cosmic Cycle of the Universe is known as a Shemittah. Like its Hindu counterpart, the Kalpa or the Day and Night of Brahmah, a Shemittah is concerned with the Creation of Worlds, the fulfilment of their destiny and their dissolution and return into the Godhead. Naturally, in Kabbalah the Cosmic Cycle is seen in Sefirotic terms, with each phase taking on the qualities of a particular Sefirah. Thus a period under Gevuric influence is stern and tough in its severity, while another, say under Hesed, is full of love and is merciful to the creatures generated in that epoch. The Cosmic Cycle follows the Lightning Flash sequence until, according to some Kabbalists, the epoch of Jubilee, which corresponds to the Sabbath Day of Rest, is reached and everything created returns to its source in Emanation again.

The duration of these great cycles is allegorical (like the 'Seven

Days' of Creation), and the quoted figures of seven thousand years for each of the seven lowest Beriatic Sefirot, with the final thousand years making up the fiftieth millennium of the Jubilee, should not be taken literally. Unfortunately, it sometimes has been, by certain writers who were trying to rationalize the concept into natural rhythms. The most important thing is that the idea of a great Cosmic Cycle leads to the realization that Time and the fulfilment of Destiny are closely linked with the purpose of Creation.

Creation, the World of Beriah, is where separation and imperfection begin. Here the cosmos of Heaven moves, and not without opposition from the demonic realms, to implement the Divine plan for the Transcendent to view the Immanent from the furthest remove obtainable. In order to do this a series of Worlds were to be created, with a set of inhabitants to invest them, so that every level might contain intelligence from the uppermost next to Azilut to the densest of materialities at the most remote end of the Worlds. The opening chapter of the Bible provides a Kabbalistic account of the beginning of the Creation of this Universe, wherein God's image is mirrored in the macrocosm and the microcosm.

7. *Days of Creation*

Jewish legend has it that just before Creation began the twenty-two letters of the Hebrew alphabet that were engraved in the CREATOR's Crown descended and stood around their Lord, each letter entreating God to create the World through it. All except the last two letters of Bet and Alef were dismissed because they already had functions to fulfil. Finally Bet was given the task of bringing the Cosmos into being, and so Genesis opens with the Hebrew words *Berashit bara*, literally 'In the beginning He created'. Alef, we are told, because it had refrained from claiming first place, was rewarded with the leading role in the Ten Commandments; but from a Kabbalistic view the real reason is probably because the letter Alef is the first in the word Azilut. It had already been honoured by being the prime letter in the World of Divine Emanation as well as the alphabet.

This folk-tale dates back to the Babylonian Exile at least; and despite its apparent childlike charm there are several important metaphysical ideas buried in it. The first is that the letters come from the Crown of the CREATOR, that is, from the Keter of Beriah, where the legend states in precise detail they were engraved with a pen of fire. This is to say they were placed there by an Azilutic process. 'The HOLY ONE, blessed be He, chose the letter Bet to begin Creation' the story goes on. This clearly indicates that we are hearing about the Tiferet of Azilut, which of course is in the same Sefirotic position as the Keter of Beriah. Considering the importance of the Names of God, whoever made up the story for public transmission did so with as much attention to

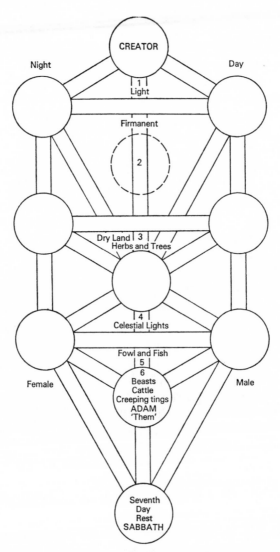

Figure II. Days of Creation. *In the first chapter of Genesis, the* ELOHIM *or the Divine Attributes of Azilut, create the Cosmos and its inhabitants. After creating the above and below of Heaven and Earth, the* ELOHIM *begin to organize the chaos by calling forth Light (middle pillar) and dividing it into day and night (side pillars). In this scheme, the seven Days are seen as states held between the functional columns and not, as some schools place them, in the Sefirot.*

metaphysical detail as the people who designed the esoteric fables of Aladdin and Cinderella. The second point about this little tale is that it corroborates the fact that Azilut or Emanation was already in existence before the Creation began, and that the twenty two letters, which Kabbalistically are related to the twenty-two paths between the Sefirot, were already well established as part of Manifest Existence. It is further verified by the Kabbalistic myth that the Torah, or the Teaching, was in existence before Creation. When the letters 'descended from the Great Crown of the Creator', Azilut was about to begin the Creative impulse. This is clearly observed in the following Sefirotic progression in the Seven Days of Creation.

Genesis opens with the statement *Berashit bara* ELOHIM *et ha-shamayin Vaet ha-aretz*: translated 'In the beginning He the GOD NAMES created the Heaven and the Earth.' This is to say that at the beginning of the World of Creation the Azlutic Attributes of GOD created the first and last Do of the Beriatic Octave, that is, the Keter and Malkhut of the Beriatic Tree. However, the next sentence goes on *Ve-aretz hayeta tohu vavohu*: 'Now the Earth was without form and void', or, as another translation develops it, 'was a desolation and a waste and darkness was upon the face of the Deep'. In the Hebrew 'the Deep' is called the Abyss. All this sets out the fact that the two poles of the Great Octave of Beriah had been sounded, but that there was between them no ordered manifestation; only darkness was on the face of the Abyss, that is, the non-Sefirah of Daat in the as yet unrealized upper Face of Beriah. The superimposed lower Face of Azilut is precisely defined by the next sentence, *Ve*-RUAH ELOHIM . . . : 'And the SPIRIT [or Wind] of the ELOHIM hovered over the Face of the Waters.' In Azilut the airy or Beriatic level moved over the watery or Yeziratic level of the Eternal World.

Creation proper began when the ELOHIM said 'Let there be light', and divided the light from the darkness and called them Day and Night. Kabbalistically this is to create the Hokhmah and Binah of Beriah, the Day being the active pillar of Force and the Night the passive pillar of Form. Thus, with the first evening and the next morning, that is, the waning of the initial impulse and the waxing of the next, the first Day of Creation was complete and actively ready for the second.

At this point it will be as well to indicate that there are at least three Kabbalistic ways of viewing the seven Days of Creation. Many Kabbalists see the seven lowest Sefirot on the Beriatic Tree as the Days, with the first at Hesed and the last, the Sabbath Day of rest, in Malkhut. These are known as the Seven Sefirot of Construction; the supernal triad and Daat being of superior order. Another school sees the six outer Sefirot as the Days on the Functional pillars, with the middle pillar of Holiness as the seventh or Will of God, running through the centre as the Lightning Flash zigzags through Creation. The last system, and the one to which I subscribe, is the view that the central triads are the six Days. This method will be set out in this book. All the approaches are quite valid, depending on which way one sees Creation.

On the second Day *Vayomer* ELOHIM, the ELOHIM said, 'Let there be a firmament in the midst of the water, and let it divide the waters from the waters. And the ELOHIM made the firmament and divided the waters which were under the firmament from the waters which were above the firmament.' Seen in terms of the Trees of Azilut and Beriah, here is a clear separation between the two Worlds. The firmament is the Beriatric triad Hokhma-Binah-Tiferet, and the action of the ELOHIM in speaking of the firmament, then making it, indicates a distinct shift of levels in the Azilutic Tree, whose lower Face is now divided from the completed upper Face of Beriah. And the ELOHIM called the firmament Heaven, which is one of the proper names for Beriah. So ended the second Day.

It is worth recording that the Hebrew name for Heaven is *shemayim*, whose root is composed of the two words for fire and water. This in turn goes back to a Talmudic version of Creation which says that God made two coils, one of fire and one of snow and wove them into each other to make the Universe. Here is another allegory describing the two outer pillars of Force and Form united in the Will of the Creator. The Heaven that was created is the World of Pure Spirit, separated by one remove from the Divinity of Azilut.

Before we move on to the third Day it will be seen that the ELOHIM principally involved in the Creation of Beriah are the YAHVEH-ELOHIM of the Azilutic Tiferet, sometimes called the CREATOR, the two Divine HOSTS of Hod and Nezah at the foot of the left and right pillars, the ALMIGHTY LIVING GOD of the Azilutic Yesod and the LORD of Malkhut, known as the Shekhinah or Presence. All these lower Sefirot of Azilut underlie the upper Sefirot of Beriah, and all except the Beriatic Daat work through the pure spirits of the Archangels that emanate from the HOSTS of YAHVEH and ELOHIM. Thus there began to be the separated intelligences that were to inhabit Heaven and the subsequent Worlds.

On the third Day of Creation the ELOHIM gathered 'the waters under the Heaven', that is, under the triad Hokhmah-Binah-Tiferet, into one place, defined by the triad Hesed-Tiferet-Gevurah, and dry land appeared. Now if one looks at this particular triad on the Beriatic Tree it will be seen that it lies quite separately between the upper and lower Faces. It is in effect like an island between the upper World of Azilut and the as yet unformed World of Yezirah. Genesis goes on to say that the ELOHIM called the dry land Earth; that is, Kabbalistically it had a root in the Malkhut of Azilut, which is the simultaneous Tiferet of Beriah. It is in this place that the three upper Worlds of Azilut, Beriah and Yezirah meet. This is defined in the three levels of Heaven, dry land and seas spoken of in the ninth and tenth verses of Genesis 1. The Earth spoken of here is not our Earth, which is not yet in existence, but a divine one which creates the grass and trees that will each bear fruit and seed after their own kind. Here begin the continuous generations that will propagate themselves unto the completion of the Cosmic Shemittah. This ends the work of the third Day.

On the fourth Day, defined by the triad Nezah-Tiferet-Hod, the ELOHIM created the celestial lights that act as signs and measure out the days and seasons. These functions are in absolute concordance with the Sefirotic qualities of Nezah and Hod, whose eternal repetition and total spectrum of reverberation and rhythms relate directly to the cyclic patterns of the sun, moon, planets and stars and their influence upon the lower Worlds. Again the differentiation between the greater and lesser Lights spoken of in verse 16 echoes the two functional pillars of active and passive and of coming into and passing out of the celestial rhythms. These cosmic laws were to govern the lives of the creatures created on the next Day.

On the fifth Day of Creation the ELOHIM said 'Let the waters bring forth abundantly *Nefesh Hayah*[ot], living creatures, and fowl that may fly above the Earth in the open firmament of Heaven.' Thus from the triad Hod-Nezah-Yesod the first creatures came into being, the winged ones to rise up into the upper part of the Tree of Beriah, and those in the waters to swim below into what was eventually to become the watery World of Yezirah. The winged creatures, it is said, were the Archangels that inhabit the Air of Creation, while the swimmers were the angels that live in the watery realm of Formation. All creatures, the ELOHIM then instructed, were to multiply themselves and fill the Worlds.

On the sixth Day the ELOHIM created the living creatures of the Earth, the cattle, beasts of the field and creeping things. Here again are three orders of being, some to live above and some to dwell below, and some to move between. All these creatures are at this stage still spiritual intelligence, for there are as yet no lower levels for them to find their place and manifest. This is borne out by the fact that on the same Day, in this case defined by the Sefirah of Yesod, the first Beriatic man was made.

The Beriatic Yesod is the Foundation of Creation. It is the place where the result of all that has happened above is imaged. Thus the ELOHIM say *Na'aseh Adam betzalmenu*, 'Let US [note the US plural] make a man in our image, after our likeness', to have dominion over all the creatures that have been brought forth. And the ELOHIM created the man *Betzelem* ELOHIM, in the image of the ELOHIM. And here comes a crucial line: *Zakhar oonekeva bara otam*, 'male and female created he them. And the ELOHIM blessed them and the ELOHIM said to them be fruitful, and multiply, and replenish the Earth, and subdue it.'

Here, the image of Adam takes on a dimension other than that of the previous creatures brought forth on the sixth Day. Adam 'the image of the ELOHIM', is both male and female: that is, Adam is in direct contact with the two outer pillars and thus expands out of Yesod into the great Beriatric triad of Hod-Nezah-Malkhut while being focused in Yesod at its centre. Then Adam or the created 'them' is told to multiply and have dominion over all the other living creatures, from Malkhut or the Earth of Beriah up to the triad of Hesed-Gevurah-Tiferet, where they may find their food in the herbs and trees and their fruit and seed. Thus there was made a creature who was like the ELOHIM but confined to the lower parts of Creation. In this way, the ELOHIM could leave a spiritual guardian to watch over Beriah while they retired to the Divine World of Azilut.

On the seventh Day 'the Heavens and the Earth were finished and all the hosts of them'. The ELOHIM rested from the Work that had been made, and blessed the seventh Day, of the Malkhut of Creation, for upon it the impulse that had begun in Keter of Beriah had come to rest. And the ELOHIM saw that everything that had been created and made was good, that it was balanced, sound and complete, and so the ELOHIM sanctified the seventh Day and hallowed it.

8. Seven Heavens

Beside and behind the Biblical account of Creation in the first chapter of Genesis is a considerable oral and written body of Kabbalistic tradition concerning Creation and the Beriatic Heavens which coalesced out of the levels that the Days defined. Accounts of these celestial palaces, as they are also called, vary considerably, and so this book presents an amalgam of several views hung upon the frame of the unfolding Tree of Heaven emanating from the World of Divine Emanation through Creation and into the upper part of the Yeziratic World of Formation.

Tradition states that there are seven Heavens. Some Kabbalists place the seven on the lowest 'Sefirot of Construction', while others, including myself, relate them, like the Days, to the central triads and two bottom Sefirot. This again is a matter of viewpoint according to the scheme of Creation used. Again, some Kabbalists see ten Heavens, one for each Sefirah. All analogues, it must be remembered, are subjective.

Accounts of the seven Heavens mostly occur in early apocalyptic literature. They are rooted in the fact that there are seven Biblical names for Heaven. These divisions are sometimes seen as curtains or veils between the different levels of reality. Thus the uppermost Heaven, called Arabot, is perceived as a vast plain, or a bank of endless cloud, and sometimes as the surface of a vast cosmic sea. Taken as the Beriatic supernal triad Keter-Hokmah-Binah, it is the Heaven of Heavens, the most Divine part of Creation because it is closest to the CREATOR in Keter. Indeed, tradition uses the psalmic image [Psalm 68:4] of the Divine Man riding upon Arabot as a symbol of the Glory. A mystical account

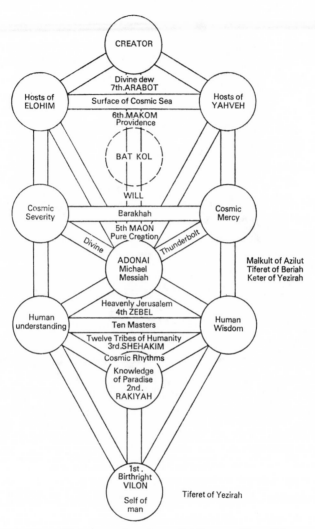

Figure 12. Seven Heavens. *Sometimes called the seven Upper Palaces or Halls, the heavenly levels define Beriatic states of Existence. The lowest Heaven is the highest spiritual condition of natural man, while those above set out the spiritual stages up through the Lower Halls of Yezirah into the Divine Presence of the seventh Heaven, which lies just below the Tiferet of Azilut. Above the Arabot of the highest Heaven rides the Glory of God-Adam Kadmon, the Divine image of Existence.*

of the seventh Heaven is that every created being cries the Name I AM as it emerges from Keter, before plunging into the Cosmic Sea below. It is also said that the creature speaks in ecstasy the same Name as it rises up through the surface of the Cosmic Ocean to return and merge into the CREATOR Keter again. If one considers the position of the Beriatic supernal triad, it will be seen that underlying it is YAHVEH-ELOHIM and the two HOSTS of GOD. This is the highest of the created Heavens.

In Biblical legend, the seventh Heaven is the place of that which is created good, beautiful, just and merciful (the attributes of the three supernals including the Tiferet of Azilut); it is also the storehouse of life, peace and blessings. It is from here, moreover, that the generations of spirits are created and return in their purest state after their descent into the imperfect Worlds below. Here too is found the Divine Dew that will revive the dead on the Day of Resurrection; that is, when the great Shemittah reaches its jubilee phase of return after completing its cosmic round. According to another Biblical legend, the Light that was called forth on the first Day of Creation and is found in the seventh Heaven is of an order that enables a man to see from one end of the World to the other. Such a Divine luminosity is said to be perceived only by those pure spirits who have made contact with the highest level of Creation after death or during a profound moment of illumination during life. This is the state and condition of the seventh Heaven that all mystics seek.

The sixth Heaven, according to this scheme, is the Beriatic triad Hokhmah-Binah-Tiferet – it is called Makom or the Place. Here, legend says, is where everything is ordained. As the overlay to the lower part of the bottom Face of Azilut, this triad is subject to the Will of the HOSTS of GOD and the Grace of the ALMIGHTY LIVING ONE. Sometimes called the Palace of Will, the sixth Heaven is where the Providence of God is supervised by the HOSTS of Heaven, who issue from this place the measure of trials and rewards to be visited upon the lower Worlds. Under the surveillance of Beriatic Wisdom and Understanding, events are created high above the theatre of their happening and long before they manifest on the Earth below. These crises are symbolized by reports of fire, smoke, biting dews and storms that will burn, of cloud, test and turmoil – happenings that at this level are no more than seeds that will mature at just the right point in the great and small time-cycles. The apparent severity of the place is due to its simultaneous position as the lower Face of Azilut. However, while it is the Divine Justice of the ELOHIM, it is not without the Light and Love emanating down from the CREATOR at Keter; and as part of the upper Face of Creation, it is the merciful and imparting Heaven to those below, although it may not seem so to those to whom Providence gives a hard time. Kabbalists, to indicate the paradox, call the sixth Heaven the Palace of Mercy.

At the centre of the sixth Heaven is the Daat of Beriah. Corresponding to the Yesod of Azilut, it is the dark Abyss out of which the Bat Kol, the Voice of the Holy Spirit, emanates to give Knowledge. That is why this Heaven is also named the Palace of Will, for here is a direct contact with the ALMIGHTY. This God Name is exactly what it means, in that the power of God may be evoked throughout all the Heavens to bring about a miracle or alter an event by overriding the Beriatic laws with the application of a higher Azilutic act of Divine Government. The special quality of the non-Sefirah of Daat is seen here in the possibility of direct intervention by God.

The fifth Heaven corresponds to the Day upon which dry land and plants appeared. It is called Maon or Dwelling. Here, in the Beriatic triad of Hesed-Gevurah-Tiferet, is where the seeds of the seventh Heaven begin to develop and really separate from the Divine. This is because the fifth Heaven is the first to be truly outside the lower Face of Azilutic Emanation. Indeed it is a pure Beriatic manifestation, lying between the upper and lower Worlds that will meet in the Tiferet of Creation. With Mercy and Judgement to right and left, the impulses of Creative expansion and contraction are united in Tiferet, so that the fifth Heaven has a special equilibrium and beauty of its own. According to some Kabbalists it is a place of colours and sounds. In terms of Genesis, it is a level where the shape, colour and variety of herb and tree mingle with the endless voices of earth, sea and air in praising God who created them. It is said that here the angelic spirits alternate with evolved human spirits in the worship of God, the former refraining from prayer during the day while the latter sleep at night. This Heaven is also named the place of the Barakhah or Blessing, and the celestial zone wherein the Love of Creation dwells. It is also the level through which passes the Divine thunderbolt as it descends to begin the next impulse to transform the Azilutic Malkhut and simultaneous Beriatic Tiferet into the Keter of Yezirah, the next World to come into being.

The fourth Heaven, composed of the triad Tiferet-Nezah-Hod, is called Zebul, which means Habitation. Just below the Malkhut of Emanation, it is the firmament of the celestial influences. Here, where the sun, moon, planets and stars have their origin, is the Celestial Temple in the Heavenly Jerusalem. Within this Beriatic edifice is the design and architecture of the lower universe that is to be formed out of the Yeziratic supernal triad that it will eventually underlie. In this celestial region, the Great Spirit or Archangel Michael mediates from the Beriatic Tiferet between the Azilutic World above, through Creation at which he is the centre, and the creatures in the two lower Worlds that are yet to come. Beriatic overlay to ADONAI, Michael is guardian over the House of Israel, which is the Kabbalistic term for the Beriatic World of human beings who live in any one of the seven Heavens of Creation. Indeed, in this particular Heaven dwell the ten great spiritual Masters who sit at the feet of the Messiah, the perfect and anointed man who is the Crown of Incarnate Humanity at the Keter of Yezirah. That is why this Heaven is sometimes called the heavenly Sanhedrin, which guides men in their spiritual evolution towards this Celestial Jerusalem, whose Temple and altar lies just below the Azilutic Malkhut of ADONAI the LORD.

The third Heaven, defined by the triad Nezah-Hod-Yesod, is named Shehakim, which means Skies. At the Beriatic equivalent to the Divine HOSTS of Azilutic Nezah and Hod, the functional side pillars create a Heaven wherein the first generations of creatures, of fish and fowl, are set in motion. These Beriatic rhythms of birth, growth, decay and death create the changing forms that are to be sent forth through the Yeziratic Daat at the bottom of the triad. Thus, while the Spirit of a creature may remain in the

World of Beriah over all its generations, its form will undergo all the alterations it is subject to in the subtle and physical realms of Yezirah and Asiyyah. In its purely Heavenly aspect, the third Heaven is where the twenty-two Hebrew letters again manifest to reveal laws that govern the levels above. It is to this place that incarnate men can rise during prayer and be instructed in the mysteries of Creation. Here, we are told, the great millstones of Heaven can be seen, slowly turning Creation through its great cycles, while the Grace of God brings forth the manna, the food of Heaven, to sustain the Worlds below. Here, too, the prayers of those humans incarnate below in Asiyyah periodically fuse with the prayers of the discarnate souls, Angels and Spirits. At such points, tradition says, the third Palace is filled with a pure light that passes down the central column of Azilut and Beriah to illuminate the twelve tribes or twelve celestial spirits of mankind who are said to dwell there.

The second Heaven of the Beriatic Yesod is called Rakiyah, like the original of the second Day of Creation. As the lower firmament, it is the Yeziratic Daat, the curtain that prevents natural man from glimpsing too deeply into the Ways of Heaven for his sensual sanity, lest he despair over the recurring rhythms and situations that will eventually bring him to perfection. For the seeker of Truth, the second Heaven, whether he be dead or alive, represents a level of spiritual experience. Receptacle for the central column and the Hod and Nezah of Creation, this Beriatic Foundation is also the focus of the Binah and Hokhmah of the lower World of Formation, the psychological Understanding and Wisdom of man. As the Yesod of Creation and the Daat for the psyche, the second Heaven is the place of Paradise for one who wishes to discover the key to himself and the purpose of existence. Here a man, on the sudden illumination of death, or on a profound experience in life, might see the destination or destiny of his existence on Earth and in Heaven.

The first Heaven is the Malkhut or the Kingdom of Heaven. Called the Vilon or the Veil of Heaven, it is the first level of spirit possible to natural man, and corresponds in an incarnate human being to the highest manifestation of his individual self. While in the flesh, a natural man may only once or twice consciously perceive such a high state; and that is why Kabbalists give it the symbolism of a veil, which is pulled back to reveal the light of the upper Worlds when the man is spiritually awake. The Vilon is drawn over him the moment he falls back into the ordinary mental state and becomes spiritually asleep. The terms Day and Night have been used to define this condition of being awake or not awake. Such an access to the spirit is a birthright. Indeed, it may be said that everyone has experienced one profound moment when everything is full of light, when even that which seems to belong to Paradise fades into an even greater beauty as consciousness shifts from the level of the Tiferet of Yezirah, the psyche, into that of the Malkhut of Beriah or the Kingdom of the Spirit. Then, and only then, do the allegories that have been handed down and set out here begin to take on reality.

Seen as a whole, the seven Heavens of Beriah are a hierarchy of spiritual conditions. Objectively they relate to the descending levels of Creation as it emerges out of the Unchanging World of the Divine. As a World in its own right, Creation is a dimensional remove from the natural and sensual state that most humanity lives in, and yet its existence has been vouched for in many indirect experiences. Indeed, the actuality of Heaven has been spoken and written about in all esoteric traditions, and in every epoch and place where man has taken thought about the origin of himself and the nature of the Universe. While the terminology may seem quaint to us, puzzling and even disturbing in its strange symbolism, the images of the heavenly World still seem to intrigue and affect a very deep part of our nature.

Heaven is that place to which we all aspire, although we may not know where or what it is. Heaven is to most an ideal, and yet many suspect it is as concrete in its way as this world. Why is this so? It is because although we may read the symbolic accounts as subjective states of delusion or vision, some part of us recognizes something oddly familiar, like a faint memory of a time before there was the present. Some of us actually sense the dim outline of a vast cosmic scheme into which we were called and created before we descended into the natural body we now inhabit.

Those of us who see behind the archaic analogues of Heaven may with effort draw back the Vilon of the first veil, and then with more effort and the help of Grace even enter the second state and so glimpse through the dark glass of the Yeziratic Daat into the Foundation of Creation. From here, the Way lies open to all the Heavens, that rise in a succession of firmaments to the Heaven of Heavens. Those who participate in this ascension through the Beriatic World can come to know their individual place in the Universe, their cosmic destiny and the purpose of everything under the Heavens.

9. *Inhabitants of Heaven*

Beriah is sometimes called the World of Pure Spirits. Emanating directly from Azilut, Creation is below the Divine but above the Yeziratic and Asiyyatic Worlds. As such, Beriah and its inhabitants act as the intermediaries between the ELOHIM and the angelic and natural levels of Manifest Existence. The denizens of the Heavens are differentiated from the Angels of Yezirah by being called Archangels.

According to the Talmud, the separated intelligences that were created during the Six Days that brought the Cosmos into being are divided into two broad classes: the Elyonim and the Tachtonim, or those who dwell above and those who dwell below. This is generally taken to mean the celestial and terrestrial levels of existence. While this stratification is a broad horizontal guide, the situation is in fact more complex. If the law of correspondences, 'As above so below', and its converse, apply to the earthly ecological hierarchy, this would explain why there are such vast angelologies in Kabbalistic literature. But let us go, as one always should in Kabbalah, back to first principles.

In the beginning the ELOHIM created plants, fish, fowls, animals and Adam to multiply and fill the World. Thus Creation and just Creation, because no lower Worlds yet existed, became inhabited with creatures of a Beriatic nature. This level of being was only one stage away from the Divine, and so they were not the kind of flora and fauna we are familiar with on earth. Heavenly Spirits, we are told, are composed of fire and water: that is, they are made up of the two Force and Form side pillars of Beriah. As such they were created functional in essence, having no individual will of

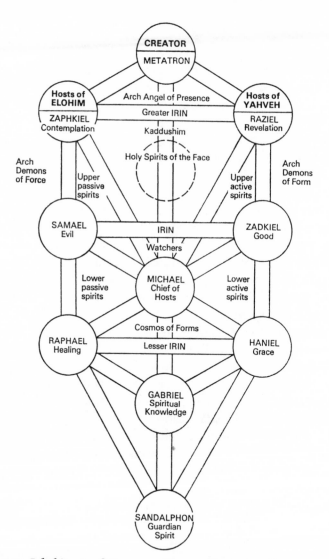

Figure 13. Inhabitants of Heaven. *The seven Heavens are filled with pure spirits. These are divided into orders of greater and lesser and perform as ministers of Left, Right and Centre. Clustered round each Archangel is a host who operate in triad and paths. Their task is to work the Universe and implement, via the mechanism of Providence, the Will of God. Outside ordered Creation, the corresponding Archdemons of Chaos test and prove the viability of the Cosmos.*

their own, because the Will of God operated down the central pillar of the Tree of their being. The idea that each creature has its own personal Tree is suggested by the male and female aspects of its nature; only Adam possessed the middle pillar in his own right, as he was made in an image of the ELOHIM. All other Spirits, having no volition of their own, had no choice: they simply carried out the directions given to them according to the Will of the ELOHIM who created them.

This concept of archangelic beings having no individual discretion is borne out by their Hebrew title, *Malakh*. In English, this means 'messenger', or in Greek 'Angelos'. They are known also as the Benai ELOHIM, the Sons or Children of ELOHIM, which sets out their relationship to Azilut. Even more precise are the Biblical terms Malakhei ELOHIM and Malakhei YAHVEH, which divide them between the active and passive pillars of Beriah and indicate their particular spiritual function.

From the Kabbalistic view of the extending Tree of Beriah emerging from Azilut, the two side orders of Great Spirits or Archangels are generated by the Nezah and Hod of Emanation. Here the HOSTS of YAHVEH and the HOSTS of ELOHIM underlie the Beriatic Hokhmah and Binah. As the implementors of the Azilutic Tree, the two Divine HOSTS create all the spiritual Hosts of Heaven. Operating through the Sefirotic Archangels Raziel and Zaphkiel, the Hosts manifest via the Beriatic Hokhmah and Binah which head the two functional classes of Archangels. The work of the central pillar is performed by a third group of Great Spirits which carry out the direct Will of the Divine. Raziel, sometimes called the Herald of the Deity, is the active, Sefirotic Archangel that introduces the first step of the Beriatic Lightning Flash as it comes out of the Keter of Creation. This Crown, it will be recalled, is the simultaneous Tiferet of Azilut and represents the synthesis of all the upper Sefirot of Azilut. Raziel, whose name means 'secrets of God', is the personification of the Divine revelation that continually passes down through all Creation. Zaphkiel, on the other functional pillar, is called the Contemplator of God because this Spirit is the reflective Beriatic principle of Understanding, one might say at this level the formalized idea of

Creation. Together, this functional pair of Sefirotic Archangels watch over the sixth Heaven of Cosmic Supervision and guard the gates to the seventh Heaven of Heavens.

It is said that all the Heavenly Host know what is to happen in the lower Worlds. Like a man on a high mountain who can see over a whole landscape, the Archangels can observe events as they unfold on a cosmic scale; indeed, their task is to precipitate them. Thus myth and scripture speak of these beings as knowing the future, or as appearing at crucial times in order to give a message or perform an action. However, it is important to observe that each angelic being only carries out one particular order and no other; another spirit has to be sent if a second operation is to be done. Three, for example, were needed in the events recorded in Genesis 18: one to tell Abraham that Sarah was to have a son, one to destroy Sodom and one to save Lot. The Hebrew says *Vayera elav* YAHVEH: 'And YAHVEH appeared unto him [Abram] . . . And he raised his eyes and looked, and behold three men were standing by him.' That is, Abraham shifted levels from the natural to the supernatural level and perceived the spiritual messengers who had come to carry out God's will.

The Archangels of the Beriatic side pillars implement the Sefirotic functions of Creation. Thus Zadkiel and Samael perform as the Hesedic Benevolence and the Gevuric Severity of God in the Cosmos, while Haniel and Raphael bring Divine Grace and Healing into the creative and cosmic workings of Nezah and Hod. From a natural standpoint these definitions have little meaning, because they are operations on a vast scale concerning matters far greater than the snowflake world of Galaxies. Creation is the World of the Spirit, and it is at this level that manifestation begins to move out of the Changeless into those fundamental patterns which all things big and small must follow as they grow and decay through their cycles. Thus the work of Zadkiel and Samael is not only involved with the birth and death of nebulae, it is also present in the emergence and disappearance of subatomic particles in our Asiyyatic World. If their surveillance were to cease or go awry the Universe would bloat or shrivel or disintegrate. All the great Sefirotic Spirits hold Creation in balance, each

Archangel adjusting to the evolving situation, altering the direction of the development, monitoring the events and the creatures within them according to the grand design set out by the ELOHIM.

Besides the side Sefirotic Archangels there are numerous other Archangels (or Beriatic Spirits) that occupy the various inner levels and triads of the Tree of Creation. The highest are those of the upper Face of Beriah, and these are in fact called the Spirits of the Face of the ELOHIM. The title is very apt as they occupy, on the upper Beriatic level, the lower Face of Azilut. The supreme is the Sefirotic Archangel Metatron, who as the highest created being resides in the Keter of Beriah. This Spirit is called the Malakh of the Presence and sometimes has the title of the lesser YAHVEH because Metatron acts as the Beriatic agent for the ELOHIM at the simultaneous Tiferet of Azilut. Tradition states that this fiery creature at the head of Creation was once Enoch the man, *Vayi-thalekh . . . et ha Elohim*, 'who walked with the ELOHIM' (Genesis 5:22). The name Enoch, or HANOKH in Hebrew, means 'initiated' or 'dedicated'. Because of this commitment, Enoch did not taste death, we are told, but was taken directly up into Heaven; that is, he was removed from the natural World of Asiyyah and taken right through Yezirah to be transformed by the fire of Azilut into the leading Spirit of Beriah, where he acts as the intermediary between the ELOHIM, the World and Man. More of his work will be spoken of later.

The inner council of the Holy Spirits is sometimes called the Irin, or the Watchers who never sleep. This is because of their direct contact with the Changeless World of Azilut, and because they operate off the triads of the central column of Creation. These Archangels include Michael and Gabriel, who are to be found at the Tiferet and Yesod of Creation, which carry Divine Will, Grace and Consciousness. Sometimes called the Messengers or Swift Ones of the Lord, the inner or Holy Malakhei impart spiritual knowledge of Divine intentions through the Sefirotic Archangel Sandalphon who resides in the Malkhut of Creation. This place is the Tiferet of Yezirah and the Keter of Asiyyah, when the four World Trees are fully manifest.

The Irin watch over the workings of Creation. As members of the Holy inner council they supervise the complex Hosts of Heavens as superior principals and inner controls that manipulate the highly delicate operations in the Worlds below, for it must be recorded that the intelligences that are not in direct contact with the Divine often strive against one another and even, we are told, misconstrue their instructions. Such events occur because each Spirit or order of Spirits sees only from its own Pillar, Sefirah, triad or path. With the Irin's supervision, however, the balance is generally maintained, except when it is occasionally upset by the assault of evil Spirits.

The demonic Spirits, it will be recalled, are the inhabitants of the earlier but incompleted worlds of the Kings of Edom, which were made and then discarded before our present World was brought about and into relative equilibrium. These remnants of Force and Form that lie outside the organization of Creation, at certain crucial periods in cosmic evolution, when perhaps the World is more inclined to Force than Form, or vice versa, attack and seek to draw off energy or matter from the general scheme for their own use, or even enter it and so disrupt its orderly progression from the Divine to its maximum extension and back again. In myth and folklore, the Archangel Michael, whose name means 'Like unto God', musters the Host of Heaven to fight the Archdemons that assault Creation from beyond the left and right pillars. Up to now Michael and all his Spirits have won the battle between order and chaos, and this has served the Lord's purpose to test and improve the performance of Creation and its inhabitants.

The minor Spirits are divided into those above and below, or the Elyonim and the Tachtonim. Some are pure Spirits in their own right and occupy the various levels of Heavens as functionary Hosts, and some are the essences of creatures or principles that are to be manifested below. Thus, while there is the spirit of the Lion from which all lions are created and the spirit of the Whale from which all whales originate, their influence extends primarily downwards into the World of Formation to give different forms to lions and whales. This principle applies to all the Spirit archetypes that will eventually manifest in the natural World of Asiyyah.

In the triad Hesed-Gevurah-Tiferet are to be found all the Spirits of the plant world, created on the third Day. Here are to be discovered the essential essences of every vegetable species not only on our planet, but of all flora throughout the Universe. Here, for example, is the creative principle of the Rose from which every rose that was, is and shall be is held. Here, too, is cosmic time and the purpose of the Rose. At this level is determined the colour, shape and size that will eventually emerge in the lower worlds of Formation and Action. In one epoch, for example, the giant ferns of the prehistoric coal forests may be manifested from this place to meet a planetary need, at another an entirely different variety of flora can be created to feed creatures whose conditions may range from one extreme of climate to the other. Each and every species of plant is here, with the seed and fruit of its own kind for its future generations. As the first of the created growing things, the plants act as the convertible and edible cosmic substance for the later creatures that cannot live, like the upper Spirits, on Light alone.

Besides the Spirits of the plant and animal Kingdoms there are also the pure Spirits concerned with the celestial activities of stellar, planetary and many other cosmic operations that work off the interaction of the creative side pillars. These minor Archangels usually perform in pairs and sometimes even in great armies of complexes that are to be seen as the working out of underlying principles in cosmic events within galaxies or atomic particles.

As well as the spirits of the archetypal flora, fauna and celestial phenomena, there are the spiritual princes over mankind. Tradition has it that there are seventy basic nations, each one having a minor Archangel to watch over it. The spirit or genius of each nation is clearly seen in world history, although we may not always recognize their character if we are within it. One people, for example, are wanderers, another are farmers, while a third may have a genius for invention; this nation holds to tradition, while that lives by innovation. Myth says that each civilization has its Archangel; sometimes it is called the God of that people. From the point of view of Beriah each nation or human group is created for a cosmic purpose so that it may fulfil one part in the cosmic role of Adam or Mankind.

At this moment in our exposition only two Worlds exist. Beyond and below Divinity and Spirit there is still no form and no body. Here, as Genesis puts it, are the generations of Heaven and of the Earth when they were created. The Octave of the Heavens is complete, but its inhabitants, including Adam, are still in essence Spirit. As Genesis goes on, 'no shrub of the field was yet in the earth, and no herb of the field had yet sprung up; for YAHVEH-ELOHIM had not caused it to rain upon the earth, and there was not a man to till the ground' (2:5). With the evocation of the dual God-name of the CREATOR and the active and passive pillars of the Divine Attributes, the third World of Yezirah begins to be called forth, created and formed. Meanwhile the Kedushim, the holy spirits of the Heavens, cry out to one another, 'Holy, Holy, Holy is the Lord of Hosts; the whole Earth is full of His Glory.'

10. Yezirah: Angelic World

The source of the Cosmic purpose of Heaven lies in Azilut, the perfect image of the likeness of God. Beriah, emerging out of this perfection, fulfils the Will of the EN SOF in creating an unfolding cosmic framework in which every creature has a specific reason for existing. Everything has its place, be it the vastness of celestial space or the most minute impulses and particles of terrestrial energy and matter, be it the spirit of the microbe or the archangelic essence of the largest dinosaur. Everything, moreover, has its particular time to be born and die. Some creatures will manifest in the lower Worlds for millions of years; others come and go in a brief series of millennia. Some creatures will live a long individual lifetime, others but a few hours. All is ordained in Beriah. Plants, animals and men have their seasons, but so too do planets, suns and galaxies, all intricately interconnected with one another, the greater containing the lesser, every part influencing the whole in a celestial ecology. All this integrated movement is created and supervised by Heaven; each piece of the cosmic system of checks and balances is set to relate one level with the next, above and below, within and without, as they pass through Time towards full flower and return. However, none of this can take place without there being a change of form; and this cannot occur in Heaven because in the World of Creation only essences can exist. Thus, in Beriah, although the destiny of each creature is determined, it cannot actually move through its stages, cannot grow and manifest the different states of its existence. Because of this a new World has to be brought into being which can allow the creature

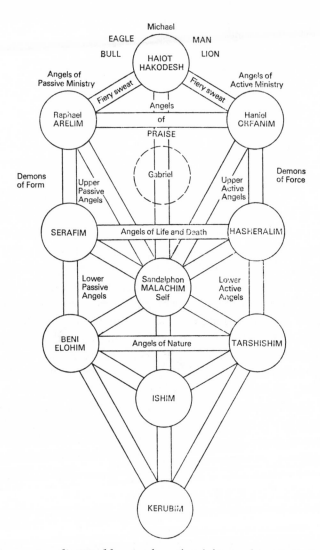

Figure 14. Angelic World. *Angels are the inhabitants of the World of Formation. Like the pure spirits above they operate in a hierarchy, but in the subtle reality of Yezirah. Their task is to act as intermediaries between the Heaven of Beriah and the Earth of Asiyyah, although they can never actually manifest physically. In essence their work is to allow Creation to take forms and so aid Asiyyah to experience the change and transformation of Creation and Evolution.*

and its cosmic role to be fulfilled, otherwise Creation remains with out a sign of change, a hint of development or life.

'And no shrub of the field was yet in the earth and no herb of the field had yet sprung up, for YAHVEH-ELOHIM had not caused it to rain upon the earth.' With this strange statement after the opening chapter on Creation, Genesis goes on in its second chapter to appear to repeat some of the processes of the first. To literal-minded scholars the repetition is the commentary by a latter-day school of Biblical scribes, but to the Kabbalist it is the emerging of the World of Yezirah or Formation out of Beriah. The clue is the word 'rain', that is water, the symbolic element of the World of Formation. It is further confirmed by the sixth verse of the second chapter, about a mist going up from the earth and watering *Kol penai ha'damah*, 'the whole face of the ground'. Here the Active and Passive pillars set up by YAHVEH-ELOHIM cause a descent from the World above in the falling rain and a rising up of a mist from the ground, that is, from the Malkhut of the now emerging World of Yezirah. This is expressed in the term 'whole face' which means the lower part of the Yeziratic Tree, for it will be remembered that the structure for the upper Face of Yezirah is already in existence as the overlay aspect to the lower Beriatic Face.

The total Yeziratic Tree comes into existence as a working entity when *Vayitzer* YAHVEH-ELOHIM *et Ha'adam afar min ha'adamah*, that is, 'YAHVEH-ELOHIM formed the man out of the dust of the ground.' The significant word here is *yitzer*, or 'formed'. The word *adamah* is used for 'ground', indicating that this Adam is not a Spirit but a creature manifested in a lower and quite different World. The seventh verse concludes with the important statement that YAHVEH-ELOHIM breathed into Adam's nostrils the *Nishmat Hayim*, the Breath of Life, and man was trans-'formed *lenefesh hyah* 'to a living soul'. This change from breath or Spirit to soul is vital in the composition of Adam because it indicates two distinct levels besides the original model of perfection in the Adam Kadmon of Azilut.

The story of the World of Yezirah continues in the telling of how YAHVEH-ELOHIM planted a garden, the *Gan Eden* in Hebrew, and placed in it *ha'adam asher yatzer* 'the man who had been formed'. The second chapter goes on to describe how YAHVEH-ELOHIM made (indicating the Asiyyatic level of the World of Formation was now in operation) trees to grow out of the ground. Time had now taken on a new dimension. Things could be seen to change their form. The Formation side is further developed into subtlety in the remark *kol etz nehmad lemar'eh*, that 'all the trees were pleasant to the sight'. Their forms were pleasing. Moreover their fruit was good for food. This is a major departure from the World of Creation because sustenance was not necessary for spiritual creatures, which had no problem in maintaining stability within a changing form. (Tradition says that the Arch-angels feed on light from Azilut.) The verse concludes with the enigmatic statement about the Tree of Life being in the midst of the Garden. The text does not, however, say that the Tree of Knowledge was also in the middle of Eden; it just says it was there. Some Kabbalists read this (and they consider every scrip-tural word and its placing most carefully) to mean that the Tree of Life represents the presence of Azilut in the central column of the Yeziratic Tree and the Tree of Knowledge represents the presence of Beriah in Yezirah. The significance of these upper World presences in the lower comes out later in the fall of Adam and Eve.

Stemming from this second chapter and third stage of manifes-tation, Kabbalists down the millennia have developed the Garden of Eden into a World of great complexity. The first common element in all the traditions regarding the World of Formation is that it is rich in imagery and symbol. This is not surprising in that its Yeziratic energy, matter and consciousness are concerned with the myriad Formations that Creation takes on as it proceeds to manifest Azilutic principles. This makes a World in which things continually crystallize and dissolve, convolute or simplify, and ebb and flow in the celestial watery element in which it is sym-bolically cast.

Constructed on the same Sefirotic model as Azilut and Beriah, the World of Yezirah has the same broad division of the two Faces. These are called the upper and lower Edens. The upper is the Yeziratic side of the lower Beriatic Face, and is therefore the

Edenic Mercy aspect to the Severity of Heaven. This shows how the laws of two Worlds coincide yet remain separate in their respective Faces. The upper Eden is the place where Yeziratic creatures come into direct contact with the Archangels of Lower Heaven. Here the Yesodic Foundation of Creation transforms and imparts the image of Knowledge through the Daat of Yezirah, and so Heaven informs, instructs and supervises in a manner that is intelligible to the beings of Paradise. Also to be noted is that the Keter of Yezirah is also the Malkhut of Azilut, the place of the Shekhinah or Divine Presence called by the God-name ADONAI – MY LORD. Here too in this same Sefirah is the place of the Great Archangel Michael, who as the Tiferet of the World of Pure Spirit is also the Chief or Keter of the World of the angelic beings who inhabit Yezirah.

The Angels are lesser but nevertheless subtle intelligences that work and maintain Paradise. Devoid, like the Beriatic Archangels, of individual will or choice, they are divided into various orders, of the pillars, of the Sefirot and of the triads and levels within the Yeziratic Tree. Over the centuries, deep studies of these Yeziratic beings have been compiled. Indeed, there are many angelologies, often using the same name for different functions. This comes about through a misunderstanding of both Hebrew words and angelic principles, not to mention corruption by sheer ignorance of what was being spoken of in Kabbalistic texts. The general principle governing Angels and their names is simple. The first part of an angelic title is its function, and the second the Name of God under Whose Will the Angel operates. Thus Barak, which means lightning, joined to EL, one of the Names of God, becomes Barakel. So it is with Raamiel the Angel of storms and Kakhael the Angel of the stars and Shalgiel the Angel of snow. Indeed tradition has it that each Angel has a breastplate describing its function. The same principle of names applies to the Archangels, but their function is of quite a different order, especially those situated on the middle pillar.

Angels are said, according to Biblical myth, to originate from the fiery sweat of the Holy Living Creatures, the Haiot Hakodesh, that bear the Chariot and Throne of Heaven. This image comes from Ezekiel's vision of the Bull, Lion, Eagle and Man, Kabbalistically placed at the Keter of Yezirah. This is the position of Michael and also of the Messiah, the Anointed Man who represents God incarnate in the flesh at the Crown of the World of Formation. In this place, where the three upper Worlds meet, the Azilutic Malkhut underlies the Tiferet of Beriah, which underlies the Keter of Yezirah. From such a combination the Angels emerge from the Fire of Emanation and the cosmic Air of Creation, to become beings that can change into any form that is required to perform their tasks in Yezirah, or to influence through the lower Yeziratic Face the upper Face of the World of Asiyyah when it comes into being.

To illustrate the Yeziratic quality of Angels, one account (Daniel) describes an Angel as being clothed in linen with loins girded with fine gold of Uphaz. His body was like the beryl and his face like lightning with eyes of fire and arms and feet of polished brass. His voice was like the voice of a multitude, which according to another source no natural man can bear to hear, which in psychological terms is quite comprehensible, for few people can face the direct intervention of the corresponding angelic archetypes in their psyches. In contrast to this exotic manifestation, Angels, utilizing their Yeziratic abilities, have been recorded as appearing in the elemental terms of Wind and Fire. They also, we are told, sometimes take up the appearance of men and women, fools and learned persons, as well as winged apparitions of varying size and scale. According to the Talmud some Angels are a third of a World high, but this observation, like the one about the Sefirotic Archangel Sandalphon, whose height extends throughout all the heavens, is an expression of their power rather than their mere dimensions. The observation that Sandalphon is taller by five hundred years' journey than any other of his colleagues is meant to draw the attention to the fact that he is no ordinary functional Archangel. His place at the Malkhut of Beriah and the Tiferet of Yezirah, where the human self is indicates, in his direct connection with his brother Metatron at the Crown of Heaven, that a very special mission concerning mankind is in his care. Kabbalistic folklore also records that despite these vast sizes and enormous powers, Angels not only deliver their message in acceptable appearances to men but often are seen or heard only by the person for whom they are intended. As Yezirah coincides with the psychological body of man, this is quite possible, as anyone involved in religious or creative work will bear out. Visions and inspiration, even if they do not originate in Yezirah, must be cast in Yeziratic forms before they can be seen by the mind's eye.

The Haiot Hakodesh, the Holy Living Creatures, besides being the bearers of the Heavenly Throne and the Crown of Yezirah, represent the four levels inherent in the World of Formation. The Man is the symbol of the Azilutic level, his image echoing the Divine Adam Kadmon; the Eagle represents the level of Yeziratic Creation, or the airy aspect of the angelic World; the Lion defines the watery Yeziratic sphere of Yezirah, while the Bull, an ancient image for the earth, depicts the substance and action zone of the World. Seen in a hierarchy, each Holy Creature is the representative and root of the four angelic strata operating from the top to the bottom of the Yeziratic World. Out of the sweat of the four Holy Creatures, thousands of Angels are generated: some, as tradition states, become Angels of ministration, and some become Angels of praise.

The angelic classes are divided according to the laws of the Yeziratic Tree. The Angels of ministration or function work on the left and right pillars of Active and Passive Formation; those concerned with praise reside on the central pillar. The angelic Hosts are also divided into nine Sefirotic classes below the Haiot Hakodesh. There are various arrangements of names to be found, but they all correspond to the Sefirotic function they are assigned to. Thus the Orfanim and the Arelim, in the scheme used in this book, have the qualities of the Yeziratic Hokhmah and Binah, while the Hasheralim and Serafim take on the functions of Yeziratic Hesed and Gerurah. In practical terms this means, in terrestrial manifestation, that, for instance, the mood of a nation is expansive if the Hasheralim in its psychology are predominant, and that it undergoes a severe period of puritanism if the Serafim are in the ascendant. It is said that some Angels are created to last a long time and some only for a brief cycle. This takes on meaning in relation to the upper and lower Faces of Yezirah. The three supernal classes of Angels have an intimate contact with their Sefirotic counterparts the Beriatic World: the Haiot Hakodesh and the Orfanim and Arelim have a spiritual or cosmic role. The angelic orders below perform their tasks to a more or less ephemeral degree. This can be seen especially in the Angels concerned with the lower Face of Yezirah, who have a close working relationship with the upper Face of Asiyyah. At this level, things, situations and beings change very rapidly; the rise and fall of oceans and mountains is a quickly passing show for the upper Face of Yezirah, which is the lower Face of the Beriatic cosmic order, and the fortunes of nations are even less lasting. In the case of the generations of mankind, or one human lifetime, the speed with which things change form can hardly be noticed by angelic beings who themselves are no more than ever-changing vehicles and messengers under the vast cosmic supervision of Heaven. And yet in the case of earthly mankind there is something different. In the individual human being there is something inherent that is eternal, that can indeed rise above the Angels and even the great Spirits of Beriah and so enter into relationship with Adam Kadmon and beyond to the Absolute. For this reason it is said that the Angels and Archangels are slighly jealous of mankind, for while they can see the unfolding pattern of the cosmos they cannot perceive God as an intimate because they are incomplete and fixed as beings, each limited to its own place. Only Adam and Eve have choice, and this gift of free will is the envy of the Elyonim, the ones who dwell above.

At this point of discussion it is relevant to mention the Demonic World of Yezirah. Like Beriah, the World of Formation has the remnants of the earlier Worlds to the left and right of its Tree. These beings of chaos, like the Archdemons at the level of Creation, seek to dismember or draw off energy and matter from the Yeziratic level of reality. While their names (and there is a whole Tree of demonic Angels, as there is for Beriah) may seem quaint to us, their effect and work is not, as witnessed in the Yeziratic Forms and Forces that manifest externally in war and internally as madness. These evil creatures, again like their superior Beriatic colleagues, are tempters and testers, and the removers of decaying Forces and Forms upon which they feed. As they have only a fragment of separated consciousness, they operate totally mechanically. In symbolic terms, they serve and work the seven levels of Purgatory, which correspond, as the dark side, to the seven levels of Paradise that are to be found in Yezirah.

As the extended Tree moves further and further away from the Absolute and the simplicity of the perfect first World, so the complexity increases, as each World takes on the Laws of its own reality plus those governing it from above. This tighter and closer intermeshing of Force, Form and consciousness is expressed in a denser bottom Face of each lower World. That is, again, why the lower is called the Face of Judgement or Rigour. In angelic terms, the multiplied number of laws is seen in the vast masses of angelic functions. Whereas it only required a relatively small group of Creative Spirits or Archangels in Beriah to accomplish something, whole armies of Angels are required in Yezirah to develop the process. For example, the supernal triad of Yezirah is the place in Beriah where on the fourth Day of Creation the celestial lights were created. This is where, according to tradition, the Zodiac of the stars, luminaries and the planets was made to come into being. At the Yeziratic level of this celestial Host, each Sign of the Zodiac was ascribed thirty armies of minor Angels, one for each degree of the Sign, and each army had thirty camps, one for each of the thirty double minutes of one degree. Moreover, there were in each camp thirty legions of sub-Angels, one for each double second of a minute, and thirty cohorts, with thirty corps of Angels within each cohort, to maintain the arcs and smaller divisions of the celestial scheme. Now, while the modern mind may find this rather archaic and even amusing, it must be remembered that contemporary science applies a greater complexity of mathematics, running to many more digits, when dealing with quite common problems ranging from nuclear physics to economic statistics. The message here is that the laws in the lower Face of the World of Formation become immensely complicated. When this Face is seen to correspond to the upper Face of the natural World of Asiyyah, then the numbers involved and their ordered division will appear to be relatively simple next to the even more involved laws that govern the lower Asiyyatic realm, outside and below the lower Face of Eden. Consider the operations within the atomic, molecular, cellular, physical, psychological and spiritual levels of a human being, and the perspective will come into focus.

11. Asiyyah: Physical World

According to the tenth verse of the second chapter of Genesis, a river went out of Eden to water the Garden; that is, there was a flow from the Keter of Yezirah that nourished the upper and lower Faces of the World of Formation. The verse goes on 'and from thence it was divided and became into four heads'. Here again are the four levels within a single World, except that in this case the World is the one that emerges out of Paradise, that is, Asiyyah or the Natural World of Making. The text continues: 'The name of the first river is Pishon', whose Hebrew root means 'to be scattered' or 'spread'. Of even greater significance is the fact that it encompasses the whole Land of Havilah, where there is gold, and that this gold is *tov*, good or the highest. In this statement, we are told Existence has entered a new phase, in that a whole or complete country is involved and that it contains the finest materiality. Now, gold to the ancients, and indeed to all peoples, is the metallic manifestation of the Divine. Gold is rare and it is beautiful; moreover it does not tarnish. It is the material closest to the image of the Unchanging Eternal in the physical World, and has been valued sometimes even more than life. The mention of this rare and beautiful metal not only indicates the Azilutic level of Asiyyah but that the terrestrial World is now in the process of being made.

The name of the second river is Gihon, which means 'to burst forth'. Here the Creative level of earthly existence is defined, and this encompasses the next level, the Land of Cush, which is the country to the south of (or below) the first river of Pishon. Like the first and second rivers, the third and fourth have locations

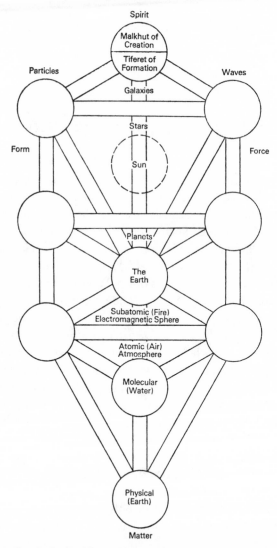

Figure 15. Physical World. *In this Asiyyatic Tree, the physically manifest World touches the Malkhut of Beriah. Thus, out of Creation the galaxies are generated and the stellar, planetary and atomic and molecular realms of the physical Universe come into being. The lower Face of a Tree, being always the lesser and subject to the upper, is inevitably influenced by what goes on above. Thus, cosmic influences pass down through the middle triad of the planets to affect the Earth below.*

indicating a definite terrestrial base, except that here the location is literal; their names are Hiddekel, the Tigris, and Perut, the Euphrates. Both these streams flow into barren countries where they water and nourish the soil into a fertile condition. Here the organic flora and fauna of the Natural World live in the abundance of the green crescent of the Land Between the Two Rivers. This is the World of Asiyyah or Making seen in ancient allegory.

Modern science tells us, not without some profound puzzlement, that energy and matter appear from out of nowhere, that the most minute particles and minuscule packets of energy when divided beyond a certain point disappear into nothing. While physicists may, at least theoretically, discover smaller units, there is always the void from which they emerge, so that they must conclude that the Form and Force that make up the material World must come from another dimension. This other World, many of the more intelligent scientists conclude, is of a metaphysical nature, that is, it is concerned not with substance so much as with laws. To the Kabbalists this is perfectly comprehensible because what is being described is the Azilutic level of Asiyyah, where all the laws are embodied in the physical Sefirotic Tree. Moreover, the principle of Emanation is clearly exhibited in the emergence of something out of nothing, just as it occurs at the highest and most subtle level of Divine Existence. Here is the *creatio ex nihilo*, the 'creation out of nothing' riddle that has tormented the philosophers and scientists, but never the mystics, over the centuries. The reason and the logic of philosophy and science cannot break the rules of the Natural World, but the mystic knows that everything has its origin in Absolute Nothing and Absolute All, which is not subject to any law but its own Will.

That there is a realm of laws which subject matter and energy to patterns of behaviour is accepted by science, although as yet only a few scientists think metaphysically. These laws manifest, as would be expected, in concurrence with the laws embodied in the Asiyyatic Tree. Thus the physical world is made up of the interplay of physical energy and matter, or the relationship between Asiyyatic Force and Form. At this fundamental level, physicists are not quite sure what to make of the active and passive

principles, and use the wave and particle theories on alternate days
to explain physical phenomena from the point of view of each
Asiyyatic pillar. The third factor, of the middle pillar, is often
missed in scientific observation, but at least the relative balance
between Force and Form is recognized in the study of the atom.

An atom is composed of three types of particle: electrons,
protons and neutrons. The electron is negatively charged with
energy, the proton positively and the neutron has no charge at all.
Here, in the basic unit that makes the physical universe, are the
principles of the three pillars at work. According to modern findings, the hydrogen atom is the simplest and first unit to emerge
from nothing into manifestation. Out of empty space, hydrogen
atoms are created to make vast fields of gas millions of miles
across. Here, the physical World's Azilutic level emanates out of
the upper Worlds of Yezirah and Beriah, the creative level of
physical existence; that is, the reality of substance is radiated from
the metaphysical state of Fire into that of Air or gas. The processes
continue when the laws of the Yeziratic or watery level of Asiyyah
come into operation. In this, the great clouds of hydrogen begin
to take on form and flow, as they at first congregate by natural
and mutual attraction, and then start to turn into simple spirals
that rotate round a common centre. These nebulae, we are told,
in time become more complex as they enter fully into the laws
of the Yeziratic level of the World of Making.

A mass of hydrogen in space, on being whirled and more closely
compacted by its own gravity, comes to form, over a long period,
dense nodules of cloud that slowly compress its component atoms
so intensely that deep pressure furnaces of heat are generated.
These foci eventually become so intense under the weight of
cosmic Force and Form that they ignite in an atomic nuclear
transformation so that the hydrogen atoms change their fundamental nature, to become atoms of helium which have two electrons instead of one. Such an event increases the weight of the
substance being created in the physical Universe and triggers the
reaction in which atoms are continually being transformed into
heavier and more complex elements. Such is the law governing
the creation of increasingly dense matter and constricted energy

that the chain of elements organizes itself into a series of recognizable octaves of weight and construction known to scientists as the Periodic Table.

The events described above take place in the smallest and greatest units of materiality and energy. At one end are the great turning galaxies and at the other the infinitesimal whirlings of the electrons about the nucleus of the atom. Both are expressions of Asiyyatic Creation emerging out of Asiyyatic Emanation and into the form and materiality that is the ground base of physical existence.

With the passing of vast aeons of time, the atomic or Creative level of the universe underwent another change, and this was the beginning of chemical action. Here, different pure elements combined to make yet larger and more complex units known as molecules. In this level, a continuous interchange between various combinations of elements went on. The grades of molecular complexity are not infinite, but are considerably greater in number than the range of pure atomic elements. The number of individual elements that may be involved in one giant molecule, with their various amounts of electrons, neutrons and protons engaged, can create an enormous complex. Here is an example of the interweaving of primary and secondary laws as things become more mixed and dense.

On the astronomical level of physical creation, the galactic processes generated myriads of atomic foci, the stars, which produced in time atomic, chemical and physical offspring or satellites. These non-luminous bodies rotated round the nucleus of their parent star and formed planetary systems. In the case of our own solar system, several planets of varying sizes and chemical states came to orbit the sun in a delicately balanced order of speed and distance according to their relationship with the solar mass. This physical arrangement has continually changed over millions of years as the solar system has slowly evolved upwards through the four levels of Asiyyah.

Taking just our own planet Earth, the same evolutionary situation occurs in miniature. The Earth, which is composed of atoms and molecules, had originally been part of the sun. As such, it was first emanated in the fiery processes that were eventually to create a cloud of cooling gas that was to coalesce into a liquid, then a solid metallic and mineral ball orbiting its star. After a long period of growing cold, the Earth's interior gradually stratified into a sphere in which the heaviest metallic elements congregated at the centre, with the lighter minerals on the surface. Over this solid core floated what minerals and elements were still in a liquid state, while above hot gaseous winds roared as heat dissipated into space and light from the sun beat down. In time, the earthly ball cooled enough to turn its four levels of solid, liquid, gas and radiation into the relatively mild elemental states of Earth, Water, Air and Fire. This stage was the final phase of the Creative Descent. Here was the Malkhut of Asiyyah, the lowest Sefirah of the four Worlds, the last rung of Jacob's Ladder. At this place was the turning point, the next major step in the evolutionary return up the extended Great Tree of Existence to the Absolute. It came in the shift from the slow metallic and mineral inorganic consciousness of the Universe into the quickening awareness of organic life which first revealed itself in the manifestation of plants which the Earth brought forth on the third Day of Creation.

12. Asiyyah: Natural World

PLANTS

After millions of years of purely elemental existence, organic life came to the planet Earth about 4,000 million years ago. How is not known to scientists, although they speculate that its arrival was aided by cosmic rays coming down from the celestial worlds, penetrating the primeval seas to mutate some of the molecular compounds into a condition that prepared the seed-bed for life. Whatever happened, it was of a totally different order to what had been, because in the Yeziratic level of chemistry a new creation was called forth out of apparently dead matter. This creation, born in the mineral-soup oceans of the primitive Earth, was a simple organism that began to reproduce itself, something no other thing had done. In time, perhaps millions more years, the oceans slowly became permeated by the humble plant bacteria. Being under the two great impulses of Creation and Evolution that descend and ascend the Sefirotic Tree of the Universe, they began to complicate and specialize until they transformed from the semi-molecular stage into a true cellular organism.

To illustrate the workings of Sefirotic law even at this primitive level, let us look at the structure of the cell which is the building brick of all organic life. Deoxyribonucleic acid, known as DNA, forms the base of the cell in the image of a double chain of molecules that spirals round itself. Here are the active and passive pillars. These chains in turn make the delicate filaments of the genes which form the active and passive pairs of chromosomes in the nucleus of the cell. The whole life of the organism is the interplay between energy and matter, with a dim sense of living

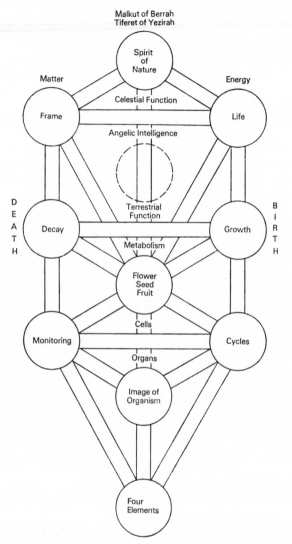

Figure 16. Organic Life. *Within the physical world, cellular life exists according to the laws of the Asiyyatic Tree. Originating from the Spirit of Nature at the Malkhut of Beriah, the upper Face defines the cosmic role of Life while the lower Face provides the actual physical vehicle. At Tiferet is the place wherein the Malkhut of Yezirah holds all the forms of a species from seed to flower and fruit.*

consciousness between. On death, the components of the cell disintegrate back to their elemental Form and Force, and consciousness departs. The inorganic state of molecules and atoms returns, until the Force and Form are used again by another living organism.

From a Kabbalistic view, the above account shows how the upper Worlds of Beriah and Yezirah reach down into the base materiality of Asiyyah and raise its level above the merely physical. In terms of the extended Tree of the Worlds, the four terrestrial elements of the Malkhut of Asiyyah have been lifted to Yesod. In this first evolutionary step, elemental Form and Force begin to perceive, even in their faint atomic and molecular consciousness, an image of the upper Universe as it is briefly held for a life cycle in the Yesod of Asiyyah. It is said that the level above is always the heaven to the level below, and so for the elements of Earth, life represented that superior World.

Traditionally the Asiyyatic Malkhut is called the first incomplete Earth and Yesod the second incomplete Earth. The term 'incomplete Earth' is used to define the seven levels, from the Malkhut of Asiyyah to its Keter, that are without a direct connection with the next World of Formation. They are seen as states that cannot realize themselves alone and need the aid of higher beings such as incarnate man to make a connection with the upper Worlds.

Over long periods of time, although relatively short epochs when compared to stellar cycles, the early plants developed into various kinds and species. This was due to the survival of the fittest in each terrestrial location and in response to celestial changes. The terrestrical factor was determined by the physical conditions of climate, habitat, food supply and local competition. The celestial modification of the plant world was due to profound changes in the intensity and wavelengths of cosmic radiation and the shift in balance between galactic, stellar and planetary relationships. These gradual shifts in the upper Worlds were highly significant not only to the simple organisms now spread over the global seas, but to the planet as a unit, which through their presence could receive and transform a new kind of energy into a terrestrial form. For the Earth it was the difference between an inorganic and an organic state of planetary consciousness, because such an experience is as much part of a planet's evolution as it is of a man's. Within the plant kingdom a slow proliferation of specialized species increased the range of cosmic influences that it was possible for the Earth to receive. Thus, from being a crude mineral ball of stone surrounded by watery, atmospheric and electrical spheres, it became sensitive not only to the sun and the distant stars, but to the other planetary bodies that circled the sun with it. According to Kabbalistic lore, every plant has its sympathetic planet and constellation. This is not just astrological myth, but a very precise description of the terrestrial function of each species and its tuning focus within the cosmic spectrum flowing in from space. It is also an idea common to many esoteric teachings.

While individual species of plants grew more complex in order to meet terrestrial and celestial needs, the basic model remained the same. This is because all plants are, to begin with, based on the cell, which, as we have seen, operates by the interaction of the three pillars, transforming earth, water, air and light into organic matter. The development can be perceived yet further Kabbalistically when a plant is placed on the Asiyyatic Tree. Here, Malkhut is the presence of the four elements, while Yesod holds the image plan the plant is modelled upon. This Foundation comes from higher up the Tree, indeed from Yezirah, the angelic World of Formation at whose centre is the Crown of Asiyyah, which in this context is Nature. The side pillars of the plant's Sefirotic Tree aid the processing of energy into matter and vice versa, while the central pillar carries the vegetable consciousness. The cellular body of the plant is to be found in the lower Face, with Hod and Nezah acting as the cellular communication system and the cycles of flow. All the vegetable organs, such as the reproducing mechanisms, are in the great triad of Hod-Nezah-Malkhut, with Yesod at the centre coordinating the autonomic processes as the plant germinates, grows, flowers, fertilizes, ejects seed, then dies. Tiferet, at the peak of the little cell triad of Hod-Nezah-Tiferet, holds all the essence of the plant for the next cycle, which will, be it of the species lichen or oak, fill out, in cellular Form and Force, the Yeziratic model held by the nature Spirit or Angel of that plant in the upper Asiyyatic Face. The plant's Hesed and Gevurah govern its metabolism and growth and decay, while Binah and Hokhmah supply the scheme with its frame and the life principle that will inhabit it. This active input comes directly through the Lightning Flash from Keter – or Nature, which as will have been seen is not only at the Yeziratic Tiferet, the centre of the World of Angels, but is also one of the lesser Beriatic Spirits at Creation's Malkhut.

Plants are a higher form of consciousness than the Earth state of minerals and metals. Born of the element of Water, they moved, over the ages, towards the next stage of general evolution that lay above the surface of the ocean. Drawn by the light that filtered down into the murky depths of the sea, some plants gradually climbed the sunken slopes of the ocean basins to break into the upper world of pure Air. This impulse towards the higher is inherent in all Creation and reflects the deep wish in everything to reach back to its Creator. Minerals and metals were lifted closer to their Maker through being embodied in plants, and plants in turn sought to climb the next step in their stage of the great cosmic cycle. Creeping up the shores of the dry land, the vegetable kingdom slowly spread over the wind-blown plains and mountains as the plants began to develop better organs for breathing and receiving directly, for them, the Air and Fire of Heaven. In time, whole new species were generated out of the several main lines of plants that had established colonies on the shore line. Some types of flora remained by the sea, half in, half out of two elemental Worlds, but others, over millions of years, adapted their standard design into roots, branches, leaves and fruit for a totally new set of conditions. These adaptations had to meet the more rapidly changing aerial weather and the more intense fiery radiations streaming down from an unshielded sky. The Earth, at around the time that the plants were climbing out of the sea, underwent another lift in level, and this was the advent of the animal, the next step in the evolutionary ladder.

ANIMALS

At one time there were no true plants or animals, just a primitive form of life. But at some point there began to be a differentiation within organic life when some of the more sophisticated organisms found they could reduce their food-gathering efforts by absorbing other organisms that had already processed the minerals needed for life-maintenance into their cellular structure. These cannibal creatures, moreover, developed the need to move on, because they could not survive in an area where they had consumed every-thing edible. At this moment it is important to note the major Kabbalistic principle of Providence. Now Providence means exactly what it says: that is, Heaven provides in advance what is needed. Thus everything in the Created Universe is in its place, and as it manifests in upper and lower Worlds so it is supplied with all its requirements for the cosmic task it has to perform. Thus, before the animal kingdom could come into being in the Universe, the hot sun and planets had to coalesce and cool into globes that were set (at this period in time) at a particular distance one from the other so that there was a temperate zone somewhere between Venus and Mars for organic life to exist in. The placing is exact, for a few million miles either way and the conditions would be too hot or too cold for cellular beings. So it came to be, at a particular point in the Earth's existence, that it was possible for organic life to be supported. The sun cools in its middle life, and so at one time it might have been Mars that occupied this temperate zone; and at another time Venus may yet fulfil the same function for the solar system, which may need at least one of its planets to support organic existence, just as the presence of yeast is vital in the baking of bread. At any rate, the conditions on our planet were long in preparation, and eventually the right and precise moment came for the new level of organic existence to emerge.

The first animals were microscopic and shared the primal seas with the plant kingdom. In time they became specialized, as they began to eat each other as well as the flora about them. Like the plants, they went through an evolutionary progression into lower and higher species, and some animals even to this day remain half plant-like despite their enormous size relative to their remote ancestors. The sponge is an example of this. All the earlier animals were sea creatures; some were relatively static on the pillar of Form, like the coral, while others developed the active pillar as did the molluscs, which like the primordial tribolite are nevertheless still fairly elementary in their composition. As the impulse to ascend and evolve rose up the Sefirotic Tree of the animal kingdom, so the government of the individual creature by the autonomic nervous system, centred in Yesod, shifted up to a central nervous system that evolved in Tiferet. Thus the animal kingdom, while based upon the cellular model of the lower vegetable Face, had a higher level of consciousness than plants whose Tiferet was confined to the very limited range of where their seed fell. In animals, the vegetable process of fertilization did not need random water or air currents or passing creatures to pollinate. Their central nervous system gave them the mobility to court as well as hunt, and so again the survival of the most canny and adaptable improved the species as the weak died and did not propagate.

Set on the Tree, the Sefirotic model of the animal was superficially not unlike that of the plants because of the basis of the cell. Animals absorb, excrete, breathe and reproduce; their metabolism is through blood instead of sap, but the process is the same. The chief difference is that an animal, being centred in the Asiyyatic Tiferet, has direct contact with the Daat of its body. In this way it is aware of its own Force and Form, its growth, prime and ageing process, from an individual viewpoint, as against the general view that plants have of their kind. This led to the development of relationships between animals, as individual creatures saw themselves in contests of big and small, friend and foe, young and mature, male and female. This generated a kingdom of an order that no forest of oaks had ever experienced, because animal mobility and sensitivity allowed flexible grouping, pairings and social patterns. Such colonies of animals, whether close communities or sparsely scattered families, spread all over the globe to make a second terrestrial web of organic consciousness. Moreover, they

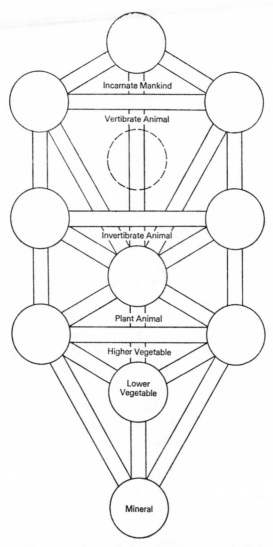

Incarnate Mankind

Vertibrate Animal

Invertibrate Animal

Plant Animal

Higher Vegetable

Lower
Vegetable

Mineral

Figure 17. Nature.   *Evolving from the mineral level of experience, the crucial interval of Yesod is bridged by the first vegetable. Above, Evolution progresses through the seven levels of Asiyyah. With Mankind comes a direct contact with the next World. This makes a human being, who contains all the stages below, into what is called a 'Complete Earth'. Such an Asiyyatic privilege obliges Mankind to act as transformer between the upper and lower Worlds.*

developed in layers, from the creatures of the bottom of the ocean up through the depths of molluscs, fish and the myriads of animals that live by the shore, through the band of amphibian creatures, to the first true land animals. These layers took millions of years to evolve, each epoch creating an advance in sophistication, serving both the creatures' need for adaptation to environment and the need of the Earth to have better organic instruments with which to transform the influx pouring down from the Heavens. Over certain ages insects reigned supreme, then reptiles and then mammals, each group of creatures fulfilling its cosmic purpose as the Earth evolved through its rising levels of invertebrate and later vertebrate collective consciousness.

Looking at the Sefirotic Tree of the animal kingdom, we see that the upper Face is purely animal, the lower Face still vegetable. The chief difference between the two kingdoms is that the consciousness of the animal is manifest in Daat, which lies just below the Wisdom and Understanding of the natural Asiyyatic World. The animal has a brain, whereby memories are stored in the organic Force and Form that make up its being. Thus an animal can reason to a greater or lesser degree with its nervous system and in some cases even dream, have images flash through its Daat to frighten or pleasure its central nervous system at Tiferet. However, no matter how well developed its brain, no animal can bypass the angelic being at its Keter. Here resides the archetypal Spirit of its species, the Great Tiger or Bear that was created in Beriah.

Animals may inhabit the Earth for millions of years, but they have no power to change the conditions they live in. They exist in a tightly balanced ecology that is continually shifting its emphasis so that redundant creatures are no longer supported, while new ones formed to meet the time are born. These, all having been foreseen by Providence, which supervises the Worlds below, are the Asiyyatic physical manifestation of Yeziratic Formations of models already created in the World of Beriah. Thus the Great Brontosaurus and the Great Dodo still exist, but now only as the original Spirits – or perhaps even at this moment their forms are being evolved on another planet somewhere in the universe that has reached that level of terrestrial evolution.

The Garden of Eden, with all the Yeziratic forms of its flora and fauna, is gradually being made manifest in Asiyyah. Slowly but surely the seven stages of the incomplete Earths are being filled, as evolutionary levels divide into mineral, lower vegetable, higher vegetable, plant-animal, invertebrate and vertebrate – and eventually man, who up to this point in our exposition has not descended from Eden.

Asiyyah, the physical World, is created out of nothing, its particles and waves composing the building blocks upon which all the physical elements are based. This atomic level is paired, despite its minuteness, with the level of the galaxies and sun, and so whatever happens in the smallest affects the greatest, and whatever occurs in the stellar Worlds influences the atomic. Likewise, the molecular realm has a correlation with the planets, which are composed of molecular arrangements. This planet-molecule interaction operates on the chemical level, including within its field all the atomic and electromagnetic factors that underlie the life on, say, our planetary surface. Again, the above-and-below pairing process or the Law of Correspondences, is observed on the level of the cell, where Nature acts as the ruler of all cells and the Form bodies they build to hold the active Force of life. Containing and being contained, mutually influencing the great or the minute, all the levels within Asiyyah carry the consciousness and will of the middle pillar as organic and inorganic materiality slowly reaches back to the Source of Itself.

The species of plant and animal come and go in the lower Face of Asiyyah, each generation but a brief organic manifestation of the Spirit of its archetype. Each species is destined to realize and raise the consciousness of the planet, before it dies and dissolves its Force and Form back into the Earth again. For this reason, organic life is called 'incomplete', because it cannot sustain consciousness beyond the cellular body, cannot bring down anything higher than the general laws of Nature, which preside over the Crown of Asiyyah. This is because even Nature is fixed. Great Spirit that Nature is, with all its angelic hosts to mould and make every plant and animal, it still cannot actually descend below the Asiyyatic Crown to directly inhabit or experience the Earth, or

lift up its being from its fixed position in the four Worlds, to perceive God and aid God to see God. This task has to be carried out
by a unique creature who can penetrate the veil between the
natural and the supernatural Worlds. The way in which this semi-
angelic Spirit was introduced into Asiyyah was closely linked with
the cosmic struggle between Order and Chaos. The natural World
was involved in the drama of good and evil, as the history of
mankind was played out in its kingdoms. Thus, in the travail of
human beings incarnate in the flesh, the mineral, vegetable and
animal realms experience the upper Worlds and so participate in
being complete. Such a possibility forwarded the evolutionary
pursuit of that perfection that would make the physical world of
Asiyyah consciously mirror the Divine.

13. *Evil*

The origin of evil, it will be remembered, is in the first separation of the Beriatic World from Azilut. Here the Created leaves the presence of the Divine and so imperfection begins. This imperfection increases, the further Creation is removed from the Light of the Perfect. A further consequence of the separation is that evil gains more ground as each lower World comes into being, as a larger number of laws and greater and more complexity confines the inhabitants therein. Thus, in Asiyyah, the creatures are tightly bound, and any small transgression of the numerous regulations can be painful or even cost life. At first sight this situation seems unjust, but it must be perceived that the further from the direct Light of EN SOF a creature is, the less it is conscious of the fundamental laws, and so its ignorance must be contained, to prevent it doing too much harm to itself or others. Basically, there are two different kinds of evil: one is cosmic and serves the necessary mechanical function of the elimination of waste and disease; the other is conscious, and is seen as a testing phenomenon or an exercise in self-will.

Evil begins with Creation. It is rooted in the first division from the Unchanging and Eternal. Evil is Force and Form impelled by the momentum of Creation, but without a specifically ordered direction – like cancer cells. The reason for this is that evil is generally associated with the two outer pillars, the functional aspects of the cosmic operation, without the conscious direction of the middle pillar. Left to themselves, Force and Form will go on expanding and contracting *ad infinitum*, either as single units or in an oscillating pattern that would shake the Universe slowly to pieces, if it did not explode through fission or collapse under sheer compression. Our present Universe is in relative equilibrium, but as previously stated there are still the remnants of the earlier Universes to the metaphysical left and the right of the present one. These remnants still contain considerable momentum of power and substance, but they have little or no organized purpose because their central pillars are missing. Thus these cosmic hordes perform in a mechanical manner, attaching their chaotic Force and Form to whatever ordered Force and Form comes within their range. This occurs because they, like all other created things, seek to improve and are drawn to perfection like moths to a candle. However, there is no obvious room for them in a well-appointed evolving system, and so they, in their distorted pursuit of completion, try to penetrate, break or drain off Force and Form from the present Universe so that they may gain entry to or make their own Ladder of Evolution. The motive of evil is ironically often good, although its methods are unlawful by their very disorder.

The idea that evil is inherently good is not strange or peculiar to Kabbalah. Nothing exists outside the Absolute All; therefore evil must have originally emanated from God. Why? one may ask. Kabbalists explain it in a number of ways. Some say that all evil comes from the left-hand pillar of Form or Severity, the principle of Judgement and Rigour which runs throughout Creation. The left side, for example, is sometimes called the 'bitter' as against the 'sweet' side of Mercy. This concept generated a whole literature about the evil impulse of the left and the demonic presences beyond that seem to tempt and destroy. This 'evil' left side is in fact the mercifully applied Justice of God, who in the final stages of a transgression rigorously implements severity in order to correct an imbalance, although it is not always perceived as merciful unless seen in great depth. This leads on to the concept that there are several kinds of so-called evil. The most easily observable is in the physical world, and gives an insight into the processes of evil in the invisible realms.

Any process, be it universal or local, has its laws. These regulations control the process and make it work efficiently. For example, the human body is a finely tuned organic machine. Anything that makes it too hot or cold and prevents it functioning is evil, according to *its* criteria. Likewise, while it consumes fuel in the form of food, it must excrete in order to get rid of waste matter and leave space for the next load of fuel to be converted into energy. Excretion, be it liquid or solid, via skin or organic drains, is unpleasant but necessary because without it the mechanism would soon jam up and cause the body to die. Now the very unpleasantness of the excretion is not without purpose. Its smell is evil to the creature that has disposed of it; but this in itself is good because it contains many elements and organisms that would harm the creature's healthy body, and so the instincts tell the body to remove itself as far as possible away from the excreted matter. Thus what appears unpleasant, or evil, not only fulfils a vital purpose, that of cleansing an organism, but actually removes the now useless Form and Force from the main area of a particular activity to another where it may well be of great use, perhaps as fertilizer. It is the same on a cosmic scale.

Besides the Demonic expressions of Force and Form on either side of the three Lower Ordered Worlds there is the presence of evil known as the Pit. (Sometimes the Pit is incorrectly called the Abyss, which is one of the Names for Daat, from the word *tehom* in Genesis, the Abyss over which the RUAH ELOHIM or SPIRIT OF GOD hovered.) The Pit is allegorically placed beneath the Malkhut of Asiyyah. According to tradition, its title is Gehinnom or Gehenna. The name has its origin in a deep valley to the west of Jerusalem (Joshua 15:8), where child sacrifices had taken place before the Israelites took the land. It also served as the city's refuse heap, and it was there that the bodies of diseased animals and executed criminals were brought. As would be imagined, the place became a symbol for the cesspool of the world, and indeed over the centuries a huge mythology was built up round its image by Kabbalists who had never actually seen the valley. Gehinnom eventually became synonymous with Hell, the place for everything that needed to be broken down into its basic elements again. This conception was based upon the same laws as applied to the excretions of the body, which are eventually purified by a secondary process which disintegrates and separates the unpleasant combinations of organic and inorganic into their respectively pure elemental states for recycling. The same laws appertain to the sub-world of Hell, the Pit where fouled or malfunctioning con- figurations of Force, Form and Consciousness that no longer have a proper place in the ordered body of the Created Worlds are held and purified in preparation for reuse. Nothing in the Universe is wasted.

As will be imagined, such a place could never be a pleasant one, because the beings and things inhabiting it are inevitably excessive or distorted in one way or another. Moreover, the rigidity of their crystallization must be enormous, as they are confined under the greatest concentration of laws found in the Universe, constraining them from being too dangerous to themselves and the Cosmos. Thus they are imprisoned, we are told, in one of the Seven Palaces of Impurity while their impurities are melted, burnt and blasted away like metals under a process of elemental and chemical re- finement. Indeed the symbology of the metallic and mineral realms is used to explain the qualities of Hell, with its sometimes slow and sometimes violent methods of extreme pressure, heat, cold and geological aeons of time. This is another reason why Hell is placed beneath the Malkhut of the Earth.

Cosmic evil is called in Kabbalah the Kellipot or Qliphot, which literally means 'bark' or 'shells'. The origin of this term is twofold. The first origin lies in the concept that the Universe is made like a series of nuts and shells. The first kernel is the Light of EN SOF, with the first shell, the First Crown, enclosing it. The second shell is that of the first Hokhmah, which covers the first Keter. Hokhmah then becomes the Kernel to Binah, and so on, each Sefirah, then World, enclosing the one above, then enshelled it- self by the next and lower World. Beyond the Malkhut of Asiyyah come the thickest shells, until at the very last is the most dense metallic shell of all, with hardly any Light of EN SOF within it. Indeed, it is said that only a dim spark of Divinity resides here, and that is why it is the place furthest from God. The denizens of this level, we are taught, are confined to this place unto the End of Days at the close of the great cosmic Shemittah or cycle. At the Sabbath of the Jubilee of the World, those held in deepest Gehinnom are released from their detaining bondage.

The other meaning of the term Kellipot is that anything, event or being, can become Kellipotic or shell-like if its central axis or *raison d'être* of consciousness is removed. If such a situation occurs, the demonic realms beyond the left and right pillars can gain a hold and so use and feed off the undirected Force or Form. An example of this is seen in the mental disorder of manic-depression, where the person swings from the active manic state of Force into the passive depressed condition of Form. This usually happens if there is no real central direction and the person is controlled by the functional sides of his nature. In the light of the imagery of the Kellipot, the expression 'to be possessed by demons' is not far wrong. In terms of Jungian psychology, it is when one or more functional Archetypes of the Unconscious take over the running of the person.

With the advent of mankind on Earth, conscious evil entered Asiyyah. Prior to this, no creature operated outside the law of its natural needs and the situation was in balance. The presence, however, of a semi-angelic being on Earth brought in the moral question of good and evil – an issue unique to the individual human being.

Conscious evil is of quite a different order from mechanical or functional evil. It means to *know* what is being done, and what Law is being transgressed. However, again, this form of evil is not a simple matter of black and white as most moralists think. Its agents are two quite distinct varieties of tempter. One is the tempter who knows what he is doing: he tempts so as to test the integrity of order; whether, for instance, a situation or person is really good or reliable under stress (and this is crucial in a cosmic plan). The other kind of tempter is disruptive simply for the hell of it and for his own satisfaction. The former tempter may be of a spiritual, angelic or even demonic rank, while the second is usually of human kind, although minor non-human entities may attempt to disrupt.

Of the Elyonim, or those who dwell above, perhaps the most famous tempter is the Devil or Satan. Now, tradition has it that he was one of the greatest Spirits, who fell because he opposed God. While this may or may not be true, it is certainly recorded in Job that Satan was one of the Benai ELOHIM, the Sons of God. In his role of tempter, he was sent to test Job's faith, and indeed he took Job to Hell and back in order to try his faith in God. However, it is clearly stipulated in Satan's brief that the Dark Spirit is not allowed to take Job's life. This is to say that Job, and all human beings, cannot have the Divine part of them extinguished, no matter how much the outer pillars may be wracked and beaten about. Job had that birthright as a man; and no Spirit, Angel or Demon could take away his direct contact with his Maker.

Another name associated with Satan is Samael, who is the Sefirotic Archangel of the Beriatic Gevurah. As the Archangel of Death, Samael is again misleadingly seen as evil, but as will now be appreciated Death is a cosmic function of contraction. Without Force being periodically separated from Form there would be no growth or renewal for the consciousness held between them on the central pillar. With death, the worn-out body in the lower World is dissolved, while the upper organism of consciousness consolidates its being before returning to incarnate below or rising a stage above. The last part of this book deals with this eschatological process.

Of all conscious temptation, perhaps the best recorded is that which took place in the Garden of Eden. Here begins a totally new story from the one we have been telling up to now. So far the exposition has described the generation of the Worlds, their interconnection, general topography and inhabitants. Up to this point everything is more or less in its place, with the manifest universe operating well within its design of reflecting the image of God from all the levels of Existence. Mankind, in its normal state of consciousness, lives in the form of Adam and Eve in the Yeziratic World, while below the spirits and forms of plants and animals cycle into and out of the elemental-organic bodies that inhabit the physical universe of Asiyyah. Thus the Manifest, Formative and Creative Worlds work in harmony as the Spirits responsible for operating created existence maintain the general balance in the ordered progress of this particular Cosmic Cycle. However, there is one variable, one risk factor in this pre-Fall Universe, and that is the two human beings in the Garden of Eden. They, the only creatures in full image of the ELOHIM, have the option of choice, and this has to be tested.

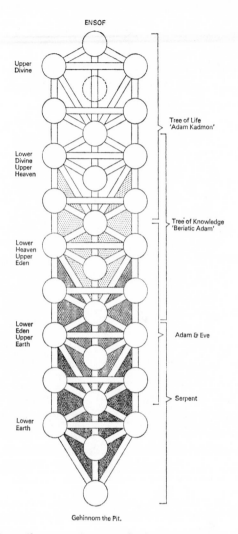

ENSOF

Upper
Divine

Lower
Divine
Upper
Heaven

Lower
Heaven
Upper
Eden

Lower
Eden
Upper
Earth

Lower
Earth

Tree of Life
'Adam Kadmon'

Tree of Knowledge
'Beriatic Adam'

Adam & Eve

Serpent

Gehinnom the Pit.

Figure 18. The Fall.   *Here, the various levels spoken of in Genesis are set out on Jacob's Ladder. At the top, the Eternal* ELOHIM *may descend, via the Azilutic Malkhut, into the Eden of Yezirah, while the Serpent can reach up from Asiyyah into the Edenic Tiferet. Adam and Eve, the separated pillars of the World of Formation, on falling from Grace, that is direct contact with Azilut, took on physical bodies as they were driven downwards from Paradise by the Angels into the natural World of Asiyyah. Below Asiyyah resides the lowest realm of Hell.*

14. *The Fall*

Adam, the Yeziratic man, was placed in the Garden of Eden to work and watch over it. Now YAHVEH-ELOHIM instructed the living soul of Adam that he could sustain himself on all of the trees in the World of Formation except the Tree of the Knowledge of Good and Evil. Kabbalistically this meant that not only was the Yeziratic Adam confined to his own world (he was not yet in the natural world below), but that he could not partake of the World of Beriah above. Now the trunk of the Tree of Knowledge is centred on the Daat of Yezirah, which allows access into the World of Creation where good and evil began in the separation of Beriatic existence from the Divine. The Tree of Life, which is the World of Azilut, is not mentioned at this point in the text (Genesis 2:17) because it was considered by the ELOHIM to be out of reach of the Yeziratic Adam.

'Then YAHVEH-ELOHIM said it is not good that Adam should be alone. I will make for him a helpmate [*Ezer Kenegdoh*] as his counterpart', reads one translation. The making of a companion occurs after YAHVEH-ELOHIM has formed out of the ground every beast of the field and fowl of the air, that is after the Nefesh Hayah-[ot] or living creatures had been brought before Adam by YAHVEH-ELOHIM to see what he would call them. This is to allow Adam to exercise the free will granted to man alone as the image of God. After this significant act of demonstration that man was indeed the husbandman of the World of Formation, YAHVEH-ELOHIM caused Adam to sleep, quite a new and lower state than that to which the man had been accustomed. This in Kabbalah is called the condition of Katnut, or the lesser state of consciousness,

in contrast to the Gadlut or greater state. Seen on the Tree of
Yezirah, Adam was temporarily confined to the lower Face
while Eve was taken from his side. Such a descent removed Adam
from the upper Face of Formation, and therefore from the lower
Face of Creation, where Adam was both male and female. Thus
Eve, the female side of Adam, emerged in actual separated form.
On Adam's awakening, that is, on his return into the Gadlut state
of the upper Face of Yezirah, Eve took up the female position of
Binah to Adam's Hokhmah at the active and passive heads of
Paradise.

The separation of the Yeziratic Adam and Eve from the
Beriatic Adam of 'them' is confirmed by the verse following the
making of Eve. Adam says, 'This is now bone of my bones and
flesh of my flesh', that is, she is of the same World. 'She shall be
called woman because she was taken out of man', that is, she is the
receptive pillar that has its origin in the pillar of Action. Here is
the counterpart to man, the helpmate. The actual point of separation from above comes in the verse 'therefore a man shall leave his
father and his mother', or the Beriatic pillars of Force and Form.
'And shall cleave unto his wife and they shall become one flesh',
that is, become a complete World in their own right as a separate
union. The second chapter of Genesis ends with the observation
that the two pillars were not aware of themselves as two entities.
They were not ashamed (a word whose root means 'to be separated') before each other. The World of Yezirah had no element
as yet to spread division in it – until the serpent spoke with Eve.

Now the serpent, who according to Biblical myth stood upright
at that time, was the most 'arum' crafty, or (the root word means)
the most sensible or sensual of beings. This upright status suggests
that the serpent was one of the entities whose body extended from
the angelic World of Yezirah down into the natural World of
Asiyyah. Put on Jacob's Ladder, the serpent stretched up through
the two lowest Faces of the World-scheme. As a part-angelic
being, the serpent could converse with Eve, who is sometimes
seen as the Yeziratic triad of Gevurah-Hesed-Tiferet of the Soul
in contrast to the Hokhmah-Binah-Tiferet triad of the Spirit
represented by Adam. This in no way conflicts with the two-pillar

concept, because the serpent meets both Adam and Eve in the Tiferet of Yezirah.

It is in the nature of the sensual always to be hungry, curious and for ever looking for excitement, and so when the Nefesh or the animal-soul of Formation, symbolized by the serpent, addressed Eve, the passive side of the Soul or Neshamah,* she was by her nature receptive to a lower but active principle. The discussion that followed about the consequences of eating the fruit of the Forbidden Tree was ignored, as we can observe in our own animal levels, because the Nefesh cannot see beyond its sensual or sensory range. While it is true to say the arguments of the body are shrewd, they are never deeply considered, as many a foolish moment of passion has shown in its result. And so Eve is seduced by the serpent's proposal, although as will be noted the serpent does not actually eat the fruit himself; that is, he was not capable of taking on the responsibility. Eve, and Adam, who was eventually drawn into the event, because he was the other pillar, suddenly realized on eating of the Tree of Knowledge that they were naked – because through direct contact with Beriah they were able to perceive the World from above, and so become aware of their Yeziratic state of innocence. It was at this point that YAHVEH-ELOHIM descended into the Garden which had been left in the care of the Yeziratic couple. Manifesting from the Daat of Yezirah, the Bat Kol, the Voice of God, asked Adam and Eve where they were.

The meaning of the question in Genesis 3:9, 'Where art thou?', is not that God did not know where they were, but did Adam and Eve know where they were? – because they were not in their proper place. Adam replied, 'I heard or noticed [*shamati*] that the Bat Kol was in the Garden'; that is, Adam on being conscious of the Daat of Yezirah became ashamed that he was not in his original condition. However, he could not conceal himself or his wife from the fact, because they now knew more than was appropriate for them in the World of Formation and so they could no

* This book uses the term Neshamah for Soul and Ruah for Spirit in accordance with the Biblical tradition of the Ruah being superior: i.e., the Ruah ELOHIM occurs first in Genesis 1.

longer live innocently in the World over which they had been set in dominion. In the interrogation that followed, the first impulse of disobedience was traced back down to the serpent, who forfeited his upright stature and was made to descend lower than the beasts of the field in the natural World of Asiyyah. Moreover, as a reciprocating penalty, hostility was created between the snake and the woman's seed for all the days of their life on earth. This is seen on the Extended Tree as the head of the now truncated Nefesh serpent, at the Tiferet of Asiyyah, biting the heel of mankind, whose psychological Tree has its Malkhut in the same place.

Because of Eve's disobedience, she would bear her descendants painfully in Asiyyah, where she and they would be placed under the greater number of laws that operate in the Natural World. And for Adam's sin in accepting the initiative of the passive pillar, his punishment was to use his active principle to earn his food by the sweat of his brow in Asiyyah, instead of having it easily to hand in Paradise. Thus Adam and Eve were driven out of Eden, out of the World of Yezirah and down into Asiyyah. Furthermore, to prevent any more abuse of the gift of free will which Adam and Eve still retained, the ELOHIM set cherubim to guard the Way to the Tree of Life. This was so that Adam and Eve, having glimpsed into the nature and laws of Creation, should not be tempted further and take of the Azilutic Tree of Life and Divinity, and so become Eternal as the ELOHIM (Genesis 3:22).

Thus it was that the Father and Mother of mankind fell. In order to facilitate the descent into the Natural World, the ELOHIM made for them coats of skin, which Adam and Eve put on over their Yeziratic souls. These skins were organic bodies subject to all the mineral, vegetable and animal principles inherent in them and at work in Asiyyah.

With man and woman incarnated at the bottom of the Jacob's Ladder of Worlds, the division between the sexes was physically manifest just as it was in the vegetable and animal kingdoms. This is the situation in which incarnate mankind finds itself today, except that since that remote event there have been individual human beings seeking to find the Gate to Eden again. Some have succeeded and even progressed beyond Eden to Heaven, and further still to the Eternal World of Emanation. This Teshuvah, repentance or turning back, was possible by virtue of the very gift of free will which Divine Grace allowed. Thus mankind, the image of God, had a chance to redeem itself and, incidentally or deliberately, aid God's Will to behold God in all the Worlds.

Whether this means that the Fall was part of the original Divine intention or not we may never know. All we can do is look at the reality we now live in. Man is the one self-conscious creature which can extend throughout all the Worlds. This implies that, while still living in the flesh, it is possible for a human being to reach up Jacob's Ladder, and pass beyond the Angels, Archangels and even the ELOHIM to become one with the Absolute. This broaches the question: What then is the full nature of mankind? Why are Adam and Eve so different from the Tachtonim who are confined below, and envied by the Elyonim who can only exist above? The next part of the book attempts to examine these questions and set out mankind's relationship to Jacob's Ladder and its powers and obligations according to Kabbalistic tradition and modern knowledge. It is also worth noting that according to Jewish legend one of the seven things brought into existence before Heaven was created was a voice that cries 'Return, ye Children of Men', so that perhaps the Fall was anticipated if not actually planned.

MAN

מה־אנוש כי־תזכרנו ובן־אדם כי תפקדנו:
ותחסרהו מעט מאלהים וכבוד והדר תעטרהו:

What is man that thou art mindful of him, and the son of
man that thou givest heed to him, and madest him little
less than divine, and didst crown him with glory and
majesty?

PSALM 8

15. Incarnation

Remembering that myths often contain as much information as esoteric diagrams, if read with insight, we shall examine the origins of mankind.

Biblical legends tell us that, when God proposed to the angelic Hosts that he should create mankind, dissension broke out amongst them. Those of the left pillar of the Beriatic and Yeziratic Worlds were against the project, because mankind would break the laws of Form, while those of the right pillar said mankind would exercise Mercy and Love. This division stemmed from the fact that mankind, being made in God's image, would have active free will, a gift no Angel or pure Spirit possessed or had ever had experience of. The Angel of Truth, for example, said that mankind would lie, because they could choose to do so, and that this would generate evil. The argument, ironically, was developed further by Satan, then one of the greatest heavenly beings, who strongly objected to the idea that he and all other creatures should consider mankind as superior. God listened to all the pros and cons, although he knew that mankind would do both good and evil. When at last the Hosts realized the significance of God's silence, that mankind was to be a special creation, they asked: 'What is Adam that Thou art so mindful of him that Thou should visit this son of Adam?' (the Beriatic version of Adam Kadmon). God replied, 'For whom is the World created with all its wonders if there is no being to enjoy them?' When the Hosts saw that God intended to Call forth, Create, Form and Make a being who would exist in all four Worlds, they praised God and agreed to honour his image in mankind. All, that is, except Satan who, with his followers, openly expressed the jealousy of the Hosts of the left pillar of Fear. Michael, the chief of the Archangels, at the Beriatic Tiferet, did set a good example by acknowledging Adam as the image of God, but Satan still refused to honour man and demanded a trial of superiority. However, after failing in a creature-naming contest with Adam, he was thrown out of Heaven for rebelling against the Will of God. Only man had the privilege of choice. No other being above or below could possess self-volition. All other creatures were to be fixed at their cosmic level and roles, while mankind could move up or down and bridge the upper and lower Worlds.

The creation of mankind, Kabbalistic tradition says, begins in the seventh Heaven. Here, in the supernal triad of the Beriatic Hokhmah-Keter-Binah, which is the simultaneous Azilutic triad of YAHVEH-ELOHIM and the HOSTS of YAHVEH and of ELOHIM, the virgin spirits are generated. Emerging out of the CREATOR's Will the Crown of Heaven, they are woven into a *pargod* or curtain that hangs before the Throne of Glory; that is, they are spread out over Creation. This curtain of virgin human spirits, moreover, is made in a special way, in that each thread or life is inter-woven with others with whom it will be associated in its subsequent existence. Thus, the destiny of each human being is in the weave, although everyone has the choice to accomplish his destiny in this way or that.

Tradition goes on to say that the untested pure spirits of mankind are made to descend to the Yeziratic World of Eden, which is called the Treasure House of Souls. Here they abide in the Yeziratic form of the soul to await their turn to be incarnated in the natural World of Asiyyah below. At this level, the soul is sometimes called a Zelem, an image; however, while it is made in the image of God, it has its own individual Formation. These characteristics are rooted in its Beriatic Spirit, which sets the special task and purpose for the particular soul that enclothes that spirit with a subtle Yeziratic body. In this as yet untainted garment, the soul is called before God in order to receive its instructions before being incarnated.

The Zohar informs us that the soul pleads with God not to be sent below into a World where it will be a bondmaid, that is, under more laws, and where it will be exposed to all kinds of corruption. Why does it have to leave Paradise where it is so happy and enter a tabernacle of clay and a vale of tears? Legend goes on to say that God, having selected that soul to perform a certain function and decided that now is the time for it to incarnate, explains the purpose of that soul's particular existence, by sending it on a short educational tour with the two guardian Angels that will watch over it.

The first thing the Angels do, the traditional account states, is to deposit the soul in the fertilized seed in the future mother's womb. They then set a light over the embryo whereby the soul can see throughout the Worlds. This Azilutic gift enables the soul to perceive those human spirits who have gone before. Some live above Paradise in Heaven, where they aid and converse directly with the Divine. Others are seen to be in the Pit of Gehinnom below the physical World, where they are tormented. When the soul is told who these people are and how they got there, by obeying or disobeying the Laws of Creation while incarnate, the soul realizes the rewards and the possibilities for a higher bliss or a lower misery in existence. With free choice and a brief on the task it is to perform in the World, the soul is then shown the model plan of its life to be lived, the people it will meet and the places it will pass through. Knowing now that its destiny is to realize the presence of God in that particular time and place within the physical Universe, the soul is then left in the womb for nine months with the knowledge that it will return at a certain moment, that of death, for judgement, reward or punishment.

Set out on the extended Tree of Jacob's Ladder, the whole process can be seen very precisely. First, a particular man or woman is created in the supernal triad of Beriah, where it cries out 'I AM' on coming into being. It then sinks through the first firmament, stretched between the Beriatic Hokhmah and Binah, down through the sixth and fifth Heavens into the upper Face of Yezirah, where the spirit puts on the garment of the soul. It then waits to transfer through the lower Face of Yezirah, the lower Garden of Eden, at conception into the upper Face of

Asiyyah and then into the lower Asiyyatic Face so that it may fully enter the Natural World.

As the soul and spirit must have a physical vehicle to exist in Asiyyah, one must be provided by that World. This occurs when the two parents come together in the act of coupling. In such a situation the Asiyyatic Trees or bodies of the mother and father are in union; that is, the male Malkhut and female Malkhut of the actual sexual organs meet in a mutual Yesodic connection. This brings the whole lower Face of Asiyyah with its organic and cellular functions into reproductive relationship as the rest of the upper body Tree of nervous system, metabolism and electro-magnetic organism becomes responsive to the Yeziratic World above, whose lower Face is the upper Face of Asiyyah. If the moment is right, and tradition states that the soul to be embodied hovers above the couple, waiting for a contact to be made, there is a rising up the central column of Asiyyah, from the sexual ecstasy experienced by the central nervous system at Tiferet, to the Daat of the body. Here, as the Bible puts it, 'Adam knows Eve', and the carnal Knowledge of Asiyyah is transformed into the Yesodic Foundation of Yezirah. Simultaneously, the Father and Mother Sefirot of the Asiyyatic Hokhmah and Binah allow the Yezirotic Nezah and Hod through to fuse into the Daat-Yesod meeting place of two Worlds, the creative Lightning Flash that is to build the body of the child and make an Asiyyatic home for the soul, which from this point on slowly becomes incarnate over the nine months of pregnancy.

The process of gestation follows the Sefirotic progression, with the single fertilized cell at Daat expanded into millions by Hesed, checked by Gevurah and centred by Tiferet, which is responsible for seeing that the embryo develops as a whole with each cell carrying the special characteristic of that soul's body. Nezah and Hod watch over the cycles and monitoring systems throughout the organism, and Yesod coordinates and reflects the evolving image of the soul's form in physical terms. This, it will be seen, is imparted through the Daat of the body, which closely follows the Yesodic image Foundation of the soul. Thus, an intelligent or stupid nature will be displayed in a recognizable form. This is not seen until long after the birth of the Malkhutian body, which then begins to grow slowly into the full Zelem or image of the person incarnated. So it is that two brothers or sisters may have the same family body but not the same psychology, may be brought up in one identical environment but not have the same philosophy of life. This difference is due to the nature of the soul, its purpose and state of development. Tradition states that at the moment of birth the two Angels who watch over the person's side pillars fillip the child's nose so that it can breathe terrestrial air. They also extinguish the Azilutic light at its head, so that its prenatal knowledge begins to dim. This is to reduce its resistance on entering this World, at which there is often much protest. So it is that the soul begins to forget the upper Worlds. In most cases the pre-birth memory is completely lost under the growing mass of flesh, sensual experience and worldly cares, but in some cases it is dimly recalled and over the years the person intently seeks the light that he once possessed. Here starts the exercise of choice between being a natural or a supernatural member of mankind.

16. Natural History

We shall never know when the first true man and woman came to the Earth. Archaeologists may search the World over but never find that creature which is a whole World distant in content from the rest of Nature, because they are looking for the most Asiyyatic evidence of human existence. Mankind comes from the upper Worlds. It was already in existence before the planet Earth came into being. Its arrival in the Natural World may have been chronologically later than most species, but this is because an organic life system had to be prepared for mankind to exist in, just as a physical body has to be provided for an individual soul.

If we view the evolution of the physical Universe, the Earth and Nature Kabbalistically, we will perceive a gradual ascent of matter towards Spirit. With the progression from mineral through the scale of plants, plant-animals to animals and the highest primates, we find that six of the incomplete Earths are filled. Each level, moreover, legend informs us, is clearly separated, so that, although the ones above know the experience of the ones below, the reverse is not true: thus, the animal levels contain the plant and mineral inasmuch as they use vegetable processes and mineral substance as a base for their own dimension. There is a ceiling, however, in the division between the Hokhmah and Binah of Asiyyah, where incarnate mankind fills the Azilutic level of the Tree of Nature. Here, the seventh of the incomplete Earths is the physical state closest to that of mankind when in Eden. This seventh Earth is the top part of the upper Face of Earth, which overlies the lower Face of Eden. This gives us a clue as to how mankind arrived on Earth; what follows is speculation.

Assuming that natural evolution had raised the Earth's level of consciousness to the highest that it was possible for organic life to reach, the solar system, of which the Earth is one of the more obvious planetary organs, reached a stage where a new faculty was needed for its development. This new sensitivity to Force and Form and Consciousness from within and beyond the solar system could only be met by an organism that had access to the higher Worlds. Nature, in spite of its elaborate variety, could not relate directly to anything above the Keter of Asiyyah; and so mankind, and no doubt this has occurred in other solar systems far from ours was manifested physically into the highest primate body already in existence. Such is the supervision of Heaven that an Asiyyatic level of organic perfection was reached in the animal kingdom that could accommodate a human soul. No doubt, although we shall never know, somewhere some of the advanced primates had strange offspring that were different from anything else that had been born on Earth. These incarnated human souls may have been a pair or many pairs, at any rate they were inevitably male and female. Thus Mankind in the form of Adam and Eve, with the skins of animals about their Yeziratic bodies, came into the Natural World. These unique beings would, with Providence's aid, invariably meet and recognize that they were of the same order. We know for certain that they mated, because incarnate mankind is the result of that fleshly union. A totally new species had been born that soon separated itself from the animal kingdom and formed its own realm.

The chief quality that the new creature possessed was consciousness of being conscious. This property was added to the experience of being a plant, sea creature and land animal during the nine months of gestation. Thus, all the stages of natural evolution were present in man besides the fact that he knew that he was aware. Such a unique awareness gave the human being something far beyond the animal pleasure and pain memory or the image of his habitat. He could actually remember the distant past and imagine the future, see things that were not yet in physical being and contemplate objects and people long gone. This was possible through the Yeziratic Yesod. Now, while animals had the Daat-Yesod facility, they did not have full access to the World of Formation because Nature stood in the way at the Keter of Asiyyah. Mankind could pass beyond the Will of Nature and participate in Upper Eden, that is, if an individual chose to do so. There is evidence that there were such people, who penetrated into the upper World, because that is where prehistoric religion and magic begin, and there are many traces of these activities in all states of mankind past and present. What is more significant is that there were obviously people in the earliest period who knew a great deal about the upper Worlds. These have been variously called throughout history shamans, priests, mystics or simply 'those who know'.

The fact that different levels exist within mankind has been recognized since prehistory. This division is not one of strength or even of intelligence but of consciousness. The earliest magicians and witch doctors saw into a world which their ordinary fellows only glimpsed or just sensed was there. Such people played an enormous part in the life of communities, and often stood in rank of fear and awe above the warrior chiefs, who only held their position for as long as their bodily strength could sustain ascendancy. Here was the distinction between the supernatural knowledge possible to man and the natural law of the survival of the physically fittest. The latter factor created an impulse that at this early time was the main driving force, and precipitated the massive spread of mankind over the face of the Earth which was the next phase of human incarnation.

From a planetary point of view, the proliferation of mankind over the globe was of vital cosmic concern in order to make the Earth as sensitive as possible from every angle to planetary, stellar and galactic influence, not to mention afford greater ability to pick up the influxes coming from the upper Worlds of Formation and Creation. Thus, mankind spread with increasing rapidity over a very short span of time, so that the human population of the World mushroomed from just several thousand to over a thousand million in a few millennia. The process is still accelerating: the number of people on the Earth doubled between 1850 and 1930. No other animal species has reproduced itself so quickly.

Furthermore, the rate of movement around the globe during this tiny historical fraction of stellar time was phenomenal. For example, in the same eighty years, over seventy million human beings transported themselves out of Europe alone. Seen from a cosmic point of view, some major demand was being met by the Earth, and the present (twentieth-century) population explosion will continue until whatever is needed by the solar system is absorbed and transformed to a satisfaction point into and by its cosmic organism.

From the standpoint of most of mankind, very little, on close examination, has changed basically since early man. Men and women still court and mate today as they did a million years ago, although outward customs may appear to be more sophisticated. Indeed, in some cases they are less so, because the rituals have gone. People still socialize and form communities with headmen and women. These may be on a national scale now, but in essence the struggle for power and wealth has not changed from Bushman times; nor has there been any major advance in government. Ghenghis Khan would be quite at home in certain modern countries. Neither has physical science basically improved man's lot. People can travel quicker, but to do what when they get there? Life is much the same once the full round of physical experience has been passed through. Modern medicine makes life longer; but what for, if the purpose of life is missed? Which it is, by those who choose totally to forget where they originally came from. Indeed, this is the state of the vast majority of humanity as it passes through the cycle of birth, growth, decay and death. Millions upon millions of lives are spent either in the human vegetable or the human animal state; and in this terrestrial condition the generations of mankind come and pass away like leaves in an ancient forest, whose long life is but a brief growth between the long winters of the Ice Ages.

However, this is not the only cosmic rhythm to which mankind is subject. Once humanity had passed beyond the herd stage, there began to occur a new phenomenon that was not rooted in tribal culture. This was the rise of civilization. While the physical base of the phenomenon was vegetable and animal security, its source belonged to something higher. Thus, out of political and economic stability, the quality of life began to change as the human race had time and leisure to devote itself to the arts and sciences. More important, however, was the concern with an upper World of gods, ideals or an overall Divine Plan, and the influence of the realm of belief in these things. Usually manifested as religion, the power of this abstract part-Universe affected everyone within the community to a greater or lesser degree as it passed through its rise, peak and then decline. Seen on a long-term scale, the phenomenon of civilization has blossomed periodically all over the Earth's surface, one bloom fading as another opens its petals to become the current focus of humanity's development. At one time it might be Asia, at another South America, then Africa or Europe. Lasting usually a few hundred or a thousand years, all the civilizations contain in essence the same teaching as regards mankind, despite their outer forms. True, they inevitably become distorted as the organism decays, but at its height every civilization is the spearhead of the development of mankind.

Now, it can be said that such periods manifest on Earth a reflection of the Upper Worlds, and this may be taken further in that the rise of great epochs in human history coincides with the subtle tides that ebb and flow in the macrocosm. If this is borne out by modern science's acknowledgement that the sun's radiation cycle can be plotted in mankind's productive activity, it suggests that the rise and fall of civilizations comes from a slow and profound cosmic rhythm. Matters of the soul and spirit are directly influenced by the interplay of the planets, the sun and the Milky Way, which are the Asiyyatic manifestation of the upper Worlds. Incarnate humanity is the link between the elemental Earth and Yezirah and Beriah. Thus, in the heightened consciousness and quality of life obtained by successive civilizations, the planet receives the influx of the upper Worlds. For humanity at large the operation is carried out over many generations, each age producing the right combination of people to come together in an organized way to perform the task. This phenomenon is not random, but based on the Beriatic principle that nations, the units into which mankind is divided, act like chemical combinations to produce different and specific effects which meet the needs of the planet in its relationship to the Cosmos.

As said, according to Kabbalistic tradition, there are seventy basic nations upon the Earth, each one watched over by a prince of Beriah. Examples of these nations are seen in the Mongoloids, the Semites, the Slavs and the Germanic peoples. The life of these ethnic groups is very long, going back to remote tribal roots. Thus, the broad Slavonic face and the volatile Semitic temperament are quite recognizable over thousands of years. Civilizations may rise and fall, but the characteristic genius of each people does not change, so that the talent of that nation is maintained despite its good or bad fortune in history. The Jews, a branch of the Semitic family, are a classic example of the spirit of a people surviving and performing their cosmic task.

How then is the purpose of these nations implemented? The seventy spiritual princes or national geniuses operate from Beriah; that is, they are concerned with manifesting creation, with each prince guiding the destiny of that people through the psychological realm of Formation into physical reality. Thus, the human race is in a continual state of flux, as the needs of each period are met by the group which is in temporary ascendancy; so that when a period of rapid expansion was needed on the planet, the Mongol horsemen performed the task, and when a new epoch of invention was required to accelerate a terrestrial process, the mechanical gifts of the Germanic peoples of Europe and North America served their purpose. On a longer time-scale, some peoples, like the Semites, carry out their destiny of developing and sustaining religious ideals while others, like the African Bushmen, maintain the intimate link with Nature lost by most of the other nations. Seen as a whole, each people supplies the Earth with a special faculty which comes to the fore in a moment of cosmic crisis to fulfil a planetary requirement of which none of the other peoples, or even the individuals composing it, is aware. At present, the Earth appears to require an amalgam of nations, and so in the last two hundred years mass movements of people have occurred all over the World, bringing about huge mixtures of cultures and races in the Americas, Africa and Europe.

From the individual point of view, the act of emigration may appear to be personal: some, for example, leave the home country for hope of a new life, some just for gain or adventure, others seek political or religious freedom, and others are just driven out or deported as slaves. But most migrations are clearly the result of a larger event whose source is in economics, persecution, war or new-found wealth. In any such movement of masses, the most adventurous or sensitive are the first to leave. Then, once the flow is under way, come the main bulk of ordinary folk who respond to the powerful impulse that drew a million or so gold-rushers alone to America, Africa and Australia, as well as driving millions out of Europe in the nineteenth century. However, although it is easy to rationalize in economic or social terms, the root causes lie deeper. One must look at the global picture to see flows and rhythms which are subject to cosmic peaks and troughs. Thus, as the Americans opened up the Great Plains, so did the Russians expand over the steppes and into Siberia, while the Western European powers invaded most of Africa. All these exploiters were technologically superior to the native peoples of these lands, which suggests that in the fifty years of this sudden expansion of the 'Caucasian' nations, a major shift of balance in the human membrane round the planet was needed. What this is remains to be seen, but at least we can look at the phenomenon cosmically and perhaps catch a glimpse of how the macrocosm governs humanity. In order to do this we must first look at incarnate man, to see how, through his make-up, the upper Worlds directly affect and influence him.

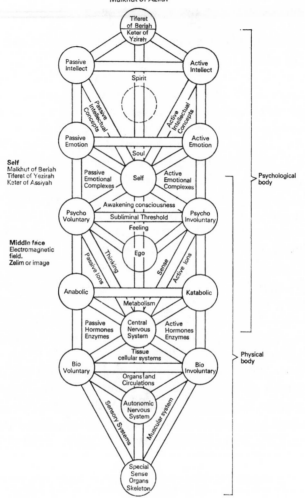

Figure 19. Body and Psyche. *Here, the interpenetration of the physical and psychological bodies is shown. Made in the same image, the two bodies operate in similar ways but in different realities. The ordinary ego-mind, it will be noted, is at the midway junction point of the two bodies and can perceive both outwardly and inwardly. On death, the upper and lower bodies are separated and return to their respective Worlds.*

17. Body and Psyche

The word 'Natural' comes from a Latin root meaning 'to be born'. In Kabbalistic terms this means to be born of the flesh. Now the flesh in this sense is anything organic, be it flora or fauna. When Adam and Eve descended from Eden into the World of Asiyyah they were given coats of animal skin. This is to say their Yeziratic bodies, which contained a Beriatic spirit, were engarmented with a yet denser body made up of an already-existing substance, form and character.

This organic body was of the most highly developed kind then existing in Nature. It had taken millions of years to evolve from the first living molecular structure in the primeval seas to an extremely intricate nervous-systemed semi-upright mammalian anthropoid. As a model, it was based on the same archetypal design of all mammals which had evolved out of the reptilian scheme, that had itself emerged from the simplest vertebrate structure of the fish. This model had a central spine with a head and four limbs, all of which were used, in varying shapes and sizes, as a standard outfit for reptiles, mammals and now mankind. The original design, of course, had emanated from the perfect image of Adam Kadmon, and so creation and evolution describes the descent from and return to the Divine body vehicle.

The working basis of the physical body is as an organic machine for converting organic and inorganic material into energy, so that during its life-span it might perform its natural and cosmic functions and reproduce itself. Moreover, the continuous generations enable a particular species to perform its purpose at whatever level it operates within the ecological pyramid of the Natural Life of Earth. Built from the unit of the living cell, all mammalian bodies are organized into a set of interdependent systems that fulfil the physical, chemical and electromagnetic levels of operation needed to maintain life. In the case of mankind, the body has developed to a high degree of general sophistication, although it cannot compete with the specialist roles of different animals. These special roles, like the roles given the nose of the dog or the ears of the bat, are not only based on the survival requirements of each species, they also serve a larger purpose in that each animal talent enables that species to fulfil a particular niche of consciousness and experience within the natural order. Thus, while an eagle can fly and see its food from a great height, it and all the eagles that ever were and will be perceive the Earth over the millennia through the eye of the Great Eagle Spirit that hovers in Beriah. Heaven views Earth quite differently through the eagle, through the whale and through the lion, whose experience over their generations adds particular facets to the Natural consciousness present on the Earth. With mankind came something different.

The natural or born body of a human being is very little different in basic structure from that of any mammal. Its chief special feature is its remarkable central nervous system. This, when set out on the Tree of the physical body, is situated in Tiferet. Below in Yesod is the autonomic system, which governs the rhythms of the body and lies at the schematic centre of what is called the great vegetable triad of Malkhut, Hod and Nezah. It is called vegetable because within this triangle and its sub-triads are all the vegetable functions of the body. On the right are the processes of Force, on the left those of Form, as matter is converted into energy or vice versa. Also found here are the muscular and sensory systems, with the specialized organs and the circulation, while at Malkhut are to be found the sense organs, such as the eyes, and the mineral base of the bony skeleton. The whole triad is enveloped in a membrane which follows the paths round the periphery of Hod-Nezah-Malkhut.

The small triad Hod-Tiferet-Nezah encloses the principle of tissues, which mediates between the physical and chemical levels of the body. This interchange is facilitated by the side triads formed by Tiferet-Yesod-Hod-Nezah, the latter two Sefirot acting as the initiating and receptive principles within the cell that may be said to be defined by the operations of the lower Face of this Asiyyatic Tree.

Above, to the left and right, are the active and passive biochemical agents to stimulate and constrain the metabolism, which operates within the Gevurah-Hesed-Tiferet triad. Here the anabolic and catabolic processes release energy or concentrate substance to be used either as building material or as stored energy (as in fat). Above this biochemical level are the electromagnetic agents which trigger many chemical actions as well as carry out many nervous and electrical impulse tasks that are needed to maintain the body in general as well as the nervous system and the brain in particular.

In the body's great Tiferet-Binah-Hokhmah triad is an electromagnetic field that science as yet does not fully understand. It will be seen that it coincides with the lower part of the bottom Face of the Yeziratic Tree. It therefore contains, with the Yeziratic Yesod at its centre, the image form of the creature. This image is imparted through the Daat or inherent knowledge of the body and on through the atomic structure of the molecules to the cells in the lower Face of the body Tree. Seen as a whole, the form field is sometimes called the etheric-double. In Kabbalah, it is referred to as the Yeziratic Zelem or image. Its origin is in the upper Yeziratic Tree which, as the psychological anatomy, contains the soul of the person incarnate. In the case of an animal, the Zelem is the product of the species, which is not much concerned with individuality. With a human being, the situation is different because the psyche is the Yeziratic form of the Spirit of that person, who was created in Beriah for a specific cosmic purpose.

The top triad of the Asiyyatic body is the level of a human being at the highest state of animal or body consciousness. Here it must be said that besides the ordinary vegetable and animal states of being there are specifically *human* vegetable and animal levels. These are defined by the upper Face of Asiyyah, with the great triad of Binah-Hokhmah-Tiferet as the human mental vegetable level, below the supernal triad which is the human animal condition. True humanity begins with the next triad, beyond the Keter of Asiyyah. This in fact belongs only to the World of Formation, and is the Soul between the upper and lower Faces of Yezirah which constitute the subtle body of the psyche.*

The anatomy of the psyche thus begins in the upper Face of the physical body: the psyche's Hod and Nezah are simultaneously the Binah and Hokhmah of the body. While these Sefirot operate as the Life and Form principles in the organism, they simultaneously function as the mental-biological processes in the lower Face of the psyche. In the lower Face of Yezirah, both these side Sefirot are connected to the psyche's Yesod, which is also the Daat of the body. In other words, the Knowledge of the body is the ego-mind of the psyche. This Yeziratic Foundation is the screen on which animal and human beings see the world about them projected. Part organic and part psychological, it is the focus of all that goes on in the brain, which is located in the Tiferet of the body.

The ego-mind is at the centre of another great triad, the Yeziratic Hod-Nezah-Malkhut. Within this are the three subdivisions of the thinking, feeling and doing processes. These small triads operate as active, reflective and harmonizing principles within the lower part of the psyche. Above is the human animal triad of awakened consciousness, which in most people is just beyond the threshold of the unconscious. The reason for this is that many people spend the largest part of their lives in the ego triad of mental routine. Only in profound moments of passion, fear, love or awe do they experience the Hod-Nezah-Tiferet triad that connects them with the Self.

The Self is the heart of hearts. It is the essence of a person. Situated at the Tiferet of Yezirah, it is also the Keter of the body and the simultaneous Malkhut of the spirit. Here is where the three lower worlds meet. This is also the place where the lowest, but

---

*For details see section 'The Body', in the author's *Adam and the Kabbalistic Tree* (Bath, England: Gateway Books; York Beach, ME: Samuel Weiser, 1974).

tallest, Archangel, Sandalphon, is said to stand to watch over the spirit of the person. The Self is also the pivot of the Soul, which rides in the triad just above, between the outer and inner emotional Sefirot of the Yeziratic Gevurah and Hesed. Below these Sefirot of Judgement and Mercy lie the side triads of emotional complexes, which store the emotional memories that initiate or retard, from the unconscious, the moods and attitudes of the person. The same is true of the side triads just above, which relate the Yeziratic Tiferet to the outer and inner Sefirot of Intellect. Here, concepts that have been acquired during life mingle with the Collective Unconscious that is present at this depth within the psyche. At the centre of this deep psychological level is the great triad of the Spirit which, it will be seen, is the bottom of the lower Face of the Beriatic World. Below, pivoted on the Self, is the circle of the individual unconscious, which mediates between the ego-centred consciousness below in the body and the Collective Unconscious that contains ancient race and spiritual memories that are focused on the Keter of the psyche. This is where the three upper Worlds meet, in the place of the Tiferet of Creation and the Malkhut of Azilut. At this crown of the psyche, an incarnate human being may directly contact the Divine.

There we have in brief outline the interpenetration of the anatomies of the body and the psyche. At conception, the already-formed psyche builds out of Asiyyah a physical body which, if it establishes itself in the natural World, proceeds to fill out in physical growth. As the body passes through all the stages of physical evolution during pregnancy, so the psyche passes through all the phases of mankind's psychological and historical development until the person passes from his primitive immaturity and reaches his prime. However, as youth and prime give way to middle then old age, the carnal body withers, but the psyche does not. It undergoes a transformation indicating the quality of that person's life. This shows in the physical body because it is modelled on the form of the psyche, and so we easily recognize the state of a person's psyche despite attempts at concealment through pleasant manners and cosmetic masks. In a protracted or chronic situation, the body permanently adopts the posture of the psyche, and so we see in old people's faces the nature of their souls. This question will be dealt with in the next chaper, which looks at the cosmic and individual balance within the psyche and its effect on humanity.*

*For detail of psyche, see section 'The Psyche', in the author's *Adam and the Kabbalistic Tree* (Bath, England: Gateway Books; York Beach, ME: Samuel Weiser, 1974).

18. Celestial Body

On the fourth Day of Creation the Celestial lights were brought into being. These were created to be *leotot*, 'for signs' (Genesis 1:14). The text then goes on to describe the making of the two great luminaries and the stars. Now in Biblical times the word *cokhavim*, translated here as 'stars', meant the planets. Thus, there are set out the *orot* or lights of the constellations, the sun and moon, and the planets, whose purpose was to mark the season and years and govern the day and night. Set in the Beriatic triad of Tiferet-Nezah-Hod, this creative combination of celestial principles underlies the supernal triad of the Yeziratic Tree, which controls the ever-changing forms in the two Worlds below. As will no doubt be perceived, the introduction of the luminaries, planets and constellations brings in the ancient system of astrology.

According to orthodox belief, astrology was never within Judaic Kabbalah, but this is quite untrue, as a few examples will illustrate. In the Talmud, there is much discussion of the influence of the macrocosm on man. One rabbi, Hanina by name, argues that the planets determine the fate of a person, while an opponent says that Israel should not be dismayed by the celestial signs because it is not ruled by any star. Another rabbi puts forward the idea that Abraham was a prophet and did not need astrology. No one in these discussions ever denies the validity of celestial influences, only their rulership over Israel, which is in Kabbalistic terms a symbolic state of spirituality that operates above the power of the constellations. Seen on Jacob's Ladder, Israel is a condition of Beriah which overrides the rulership of Yezirah.

The great medieval rationalist Maimonides was vehemently

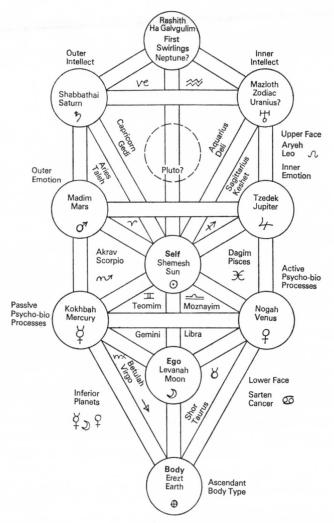

Figure 20. Celestial Body. *Here, the Hebrew and Latinized astrological correspondences within the Yeziratic Tree are shown. Astrology, a side discipline for many Kabbalists despite orthodox disapproval, is the study of the interaction of the subtle Macrocosm on the Microcosmic body of the psyche. Seen Kabbalistically, the sun of Tiferet is the Self's connection with Beriah's Malkhut, each zodiacal sign being one of the twelve spiritual types that operate destiny through the fate of each incarnation.*

against astrology, but others, especially the mystics, were its firm advocates. One rabbi, Rava, clearly states that a person's fortune depends not on merit but on the individual's ruling planet, while the great Kabbalist Shabbethai Donnolo of Bari wrote various treatises on the subject and a commentary on the *Sefer Yezirah*.

The *Sefer Yezirah*, or the Book of Formation, is one of the important classics of early Kabbalah. Indeed, it is so respectable that Saadia Gaon, the leading scholar of a major rabbinical academy, wrote a commentary on it. Its content is a symbolic scheme of the Universe cast in Biblical and astrological terms, and it sets out in great detail the interconnection between the macrocosm of the Heavens and the microcosm of man. While this is conclusive proof of the acknowledgement and use of astrology within the tradition, perhaps a passage from the other major Kabbalistic canon, the *Zohar*, will set the subject in perspective. In the section called 'Vayesheb', coded 180b to 181a, there is the following: 'I have found a Mystic Teaching in the books of the ancient ones and next to it another esoteric Tradition, both being in inner content the same.' The passage then goes on to speak about the influence of the sun and moon and their effect upon the lives of men, and how prayer can mitigate apparent ill-fortune. It also talks of the portion of *mazzel* or Fortune allotted to different grades of souls in order that they may perfect themselves. This is the basic attitude of Kabbalah to astrology. Jews to this day say *mazzel tov* at celebrations. While it has come to mean 'Good luck', its literal translation and root is concerned with astrological influence. The branch word *mazalot* means the Zodiac.

According to Kabbalistic tradition, each of the Sefirot is accorded a planet. Beginning with the Earth at Malkhut, the evocative symbolism of the Graeco-Roman gods is applied to illustrate the qualities of the planets in Yeziratic language. This astrological use of mythology does not imply belief in the classical gods, but merely demonstrates the workings of the World of Formation. Thus, while the celestial bodies are placed on the Asiyyatic Tree, with the physical sun at Tiferet, the subtle operations of their influence are described in terms of the flowing moods of Yezirah, the World of Angels – some of whom, according to tradition, watch over the planetary principles which act as intermediaries between the earthly World of Asiyyah and the heavenly supervision of Beriah. In recent times Kabbalists have overlaid Hokhmah, traditionally the Zodiac, with Uranus, and Keter, traditionally *Reshit hagilgulim*, the Prime Swirlings or fiery mist of the Galaxy, with Neptune. These last placings, like the further superimposition of the recently discovered Pluto on Daat, are only speculative. As a whole, the scheme sets out the active and passive planets on the functional side columns with the luminaries of consciousness and will on the middle pillar.*

The Zodiac, the band of twelve constellations through which the sun, moon and planets pass during the course of their journey round the Heavens, is touched on in Kabbalistic tradition symbolically. The *Sefer Yezirah* gives a precise account of the time of year and the area of the human body which they govern, and allots to each of them one of the twelve tribes of Israel. Each of this Biblical brotherhood represents one of the twelve essential types of human being, that is, the twelve Yeziratic Tiferet natures possible. Thus for example Judah, the scion of the royal tribe, is traditionally the martial sign of Aries, while Menasseh, Scorpio, is the tribe of mystics and prophets. Other tribes according to tradition are: Issachar: Taurus; Zebuluh: Gemini; Rueben: Cancer; Simeon: Leo; Gad: Virgo; Ephraim: Libra; Benjamin: Saggitarius; Dan: Capricorn; Asher: Aquarius; Naphtali: Pisces. From the point of view of the Yeziratic Tree, the Zodiac is set out in the side triads, with the signs of Leo and Cancer placed over the upper and lower Faces where the sun and moon rule. It should be noted that the placing of each sign is relevant to its ruling planet and the adjacent Sefirot. Sefirotic law is also observed in that the masculine and feminine signs are directly related to the active and passive sides of the Tree. This same Kabbalistic rule applies to the sun and moon, the active and passive luminaries which express the vertical axis of Mercy and Severity.

The interacting complexity of the celestial bodies and the Zodiac has been touched upon in the number of angelic armies,

*For a detailed account of planetary gods on the Tree see the author's *Tree of Life* (London, England: Rider & Company; York Beach, ME: Samuel Weiser, 1975).

camps, legions and cohorts ascribed to the Yeziratic operations. Indeed, detailed accounts of the Angels and the mechanism of the planetary and stellar world are to be found in several apocalyptic works, like the section on the courses of the heavenly luminaries in one of the Books of Enoch. From the point of view of our examination of the relation between the upper Worlds and in- arcnate mankind, we will look only at the interconnection of the psyche with the astrological aspects of Yezirah.

As should have been realized, the psychological Tree of a human being can be exactly superimposed over the Tree of the Zodiac and the celestial luminaries. Thus there is a precise corres- pondence between the sun and the Self, the moon and the Ego, and between all the planets and the various psychological functions. It is the same with all the triads, excluding the five horizontal ones, which are concerned with levels of consciousness and will.

For obvious reasons, this astrological-psychological Kabbalistic study is too complex to deal with in detail in this book, and so we must accept the brief formula that each incarnation of a human being out of Yezirah and into an Asiyyatic body brings about a physical crystallization of the individual spirit's status at that moment of birth. Thus, the positions of the physical planets, sun and moon in relation to the Zodiac and their configuration as re- gards the Earth act as indicators to the subtle state of the macro- cosm like hands do to a clock. Neither the hands nor the clock are Time itself, but only represent its rhythms. So it is with the birth chart that sets out the relationship between the macrocosmic principles of Yezirah and the microcosmic structure of the psyche.

An example of planetary correspondence may be seen in the emotional pair of Mars and Jupiter. Here the discipline of Mars and the expansive power of Jupiter demonstrate, in archetypal form, the control of the psychological Gevurah or Judgement and the deep emotional drive of the Love and Mercy in Hesed. To take the connection further, the archetypal image of the ancient gods in fact corresponds precisely with the archetypes found in modern Jungian psychology, so that Mars becomes the Hero and Jupiter the great King. The tradition of Western magic, which has

borrowed many Kabbalistic principles, uses the identical archetypes to evoke the Yeziratic Sefirot in their magical operations.
The psychological archetypes of the Trickster and the beautiful
Youth or Maiden relate directly to Mercury and Venus, who are
ascribed to Hod and Nezah. Hokhmah and Binah, known in
Kabbalah as the great Father and Mother, relate to the Animus
and Anima of the psyche, and their planets Uranus and Saturn to
the Magician and Great Mother of the magical Tradition. From
all this it will be gathered that the same Sefirotic principles emerge
at the level of macrocosm and microcosm, of inner and outer
manifestation. To illustrate the point, let us take the sun and moon.
The astronomical sun is to be found in Asiyyah in the sky and
biologically in the body at the central nervous system, while the
moon, acting as the giant mechanical pendulum on the Earth's
natural rhythms, is to be seen in the microcosm in the autonomic
system of the body. In Yezirah the sun is the Self, that inner pivot
that illuminates the whole psyche despite the often eclipsing inner
moon of the ego-mind that only reflects the images of consciousness.

Astrologically and psychologically speaking, the essential Self
of a human being belongs to one of the twelve types, which
correspond to the sun signs. This is to say that his or her Tiferet
has a Capricornian or a Geminian flavour. Thus, while the Self is
the Malkhut of the Spirit of Beriah, it has a particular Yeziratic
flavour through one of the Zodiacal signs. This flavour is taken
further by being passed through the simultaneous Keter of
Asiyyah; and thus the body too has Capricornian or Geminian
characteristics. In an actual incarnation this means that, in the
case of the Capricornian, the Self will be serious, slow to action,
and given to all the gifts and foibles of that sign. In turn, this
essentially Capricornian psyche will affect the inherited body in a
Capricornian way, even though the ascendant or physical body
type, set in the Malkhut of Yezirah and the Tiferet of Asiyyah,
will modify the physical character. Likewise the position of the
moon, say in Scorpio, at the moment of birth will affect Yesod by
overlaying the ego with a Scorpionic ego-mind that will influence
the person's outlook. The term 'outlook' is very precise.

Before we proceed to see how mankind is influenced from above, we must realize that the effect is in fact accomplished from within. Moreover, there are several different levels by which an individual may be influenced, and not everyone is subject to all of them. To sum up a very complicated mechanism, the psychological body of a human being is made up of the same Substance, Force and Consciousness as the World that governs the state of macrocosm. This macrocosm is not only the physical celestial bodies, but the subtle tides and ever changing forms of Yeziratic combinations. These combinations are composed of the Yeziratic principles that lie behind the mood of a time. Seen as celestial influences, they are in fact the workings of the Tree of Formation, which in turn is subject to the creative impulses of Creation out of which it originally emerged. Thus an individual who was created for a particular purpose is given a specific psychological anatomy which is tuned by the inclination of the celestial balance in the Zodiac. This particular temperament, which is composed of many subtle configurations of Yeziratic triads and planetary-Sefirotic eases and tensions, is exactly suited to the epoch into which the individual is born. He is indeed a child of his time. As such, he may choose to exist as an ordinary person amongst many in Asiyyah, live a distinct fate in Yezirah, or act out a cosmic destiny in Beriah while on earth.

19. Fate: General

We have seen, in the chapter on incarnation (Chapter 15), how the Yeziratic body of the psyche is connected by conception to the fertilized seed of the Asiyyatic body, and how it slowly invests the growing embryo up to the moment of birth. At the first breath, the fluid state of the Yeziratic body solidifies into a relatively crystallized psyche as it fully enters the Natural World via the Malkhut of Asiyyah. From this point on the whole process is reversed, as the creative Lightning Flash turns into the evolutionary impulse, to rise up the Jacob's Ladder again towards its source.

The first step is that the baby, having been removed from its mother's womb, has to go onto a completely new nourishment system. This, in terms of the Asiyyatic Tree, is taken over by the Tiferet of the central nervous system, which is the Malkhut of Yezirah or the bodily base of the psyche. As the organic process of growth to fill out the Zelem, image, of the full grown person continues, the Yesod of the psyche, which is also the Daat of the body, begins to build up an image of the body and form a Foundation for the psyche. This focus becomes the ego-mind and constitutes the lunar stage of mankind after the earth stage of body building. The Mercury stage is childhood, where Hod or the bio-psychological principle of voluntary learning and communication is brought into function. This in turn is followed by youth and the development of the active instinctive Nezah processes in bio-psychology. The prime of the person is reached at the Sun or Tiferet stage, when the individual is organically fully grown and all his physical potential is seen. This occurs between the ages of about thirty and forty. The Mars and Jupiter or Gevurah and Hesed phases represent the disciplined direction of the life and the onset of middle age with its accompanying generosity as ambitions are fulfilled, while the Saturn and Uranus stages operate the reflections on Life's laws by Binah and the revelations received by the inner intellect of Hokhmah. Daat, the principle of Knowledge, applies only to people who listen to the voice of the Spirit. Death occurs at Keter, where the individual unites with the Divine again, for in the Keter of Yezirah is the Malkhut of Azilut. If this uniting is not permanent then the Soul returns down again to begin a new cycle.★

As each Yeziratic Sefirah is passed through in psychological growth, so a particular planetary principle is contacted. This means that only those parts of the psyche that have been developed can have *direct* access to the cosmic levels of existence. In practical terms this means that the macrocosmic influence of the upper Worlds has a merely general effect on those people who have not progressed beyond a certain stage of development and consequently do not respond in a selective manner to the subtler and celestial events going on around them. People divide, by their own choice, into a general or a particular quality of Life.

To illustrate the above principle, let us begin at Malkhut. A person who lives only for the body is subject to no particular law other than that of physical existence. He will eat, sleep and die at the level of a human vegetable. Life will be just one long round of a single day and night repeating the same pattern with a little seasonal variation. He will be totally earthbound. No other event will affect him; even times of peace and war will have a minimal effect because he will be concerned only with physical survival at any cost. A person who has developed to the ego-moon phase will be on a higher level. However, for this type everything will be ego-centred, with the whole world revolving about the person's moods and image of life. Such people will be completely oblivious, as a baby is, to any event unconnected with them personally. They will be in effect, as adults, true lunatics, which is to say they

★For a detailed account of the stages of life, see chapter, 'Birth–Life–Death', in the author's *Tree of Life* (London, England: Rider; York Beach, ME: Samuel Weiser, 1975).

will live their lives entirely under the ebb and flow of the lunar rhythms. In practical terms, this might be a little more outward-looking than the Malkhut Earth state, but no more than 'me and mine' and 'us and them'.

The Mercury and Venus states are clearly seen in the preoccupations with childlike amusements, curiosity and excitement, and sensual pleasure and passions. People who stop at the Mercury state are well informed as regards the facts but have no real experience. They will view world events with an encyclopedic mentality but never respond to the reality of them, although they will compose endless theories about how to solve the world's problems. The people who reach, but do not go beyond, the Venus state have experience but no wish to see the significance of it. They are brave and will take what life offers, but they will never proceed beyond the satisfaction of desire, will never question why a good or bad thing happened, and so they run or wander from one pleasure or pain to the next without learning any lesson, until one day all physical pleasures have been exhausted and there seems to be no more to life but death. Both the Mercury-Hod and Venus-Nezah phases belong to the bio-psychological level and constitute a general vegetable level of human existence. Kabbalah calls people of this level *am haaretz*: people of the Earth. As regards cosmic events, they are subject to the affairs of the outer world and are affected *en masse* by the planetary rhythms that govern the mundane current events of mankind. This is what is usually regarded as history.

The great triad formed by the Yeziratic Hod-Nezah-Malkhut has within it three sub-triads centred on the Yesodic ego. These sub-triads are in a single individual the thinking, feeling and doing aspects of his nature. On the scale of mankind, they represent the three body types symbolized by the three sons of Noah, Shem, Ham and Japheth, who were the mythological fathers of the three basic divisions within the human race. These physical divisions are quite different from the twelve patriarchs of Israel, who represent the twelve psycho-spiritual types of the Self. Seen as a working total each triad is subject to the general influence of whatever celestial principle is predominant over a given period. Thus, for example, there will be moments of action, expansion and adventure when the Venus-moon-earth triad is stimulated, and periods of mental speculation and invention when the Mercury-moon-earth triad is activated; while epochs of art will occur when the Mercury-moon-Venus triangle is to the fore. All these phases will be seen as an ever-changing kaleidoscope of mundane moods that affect the world population in different ways. An example is seen in the sudden fashion for a particular amusement that sweeps round the globe, as the hula-hoop craze did; or the flare-up of a small war; or the brief fascination with a new invention or scientific event like the landing on the moon, which despite its cosmic significance soon lost the interest of the world audience. As will be observed, there is little individuality at this level. It is much of a muchness, with millions living roughly similar kinds of lives despite the difference in time, place, costume and custom.

Individuality begins with the animal level, the sun and the Self. Here, a person begins to be what he or she really is. There is a truth and a light present, and when it looks down from the human-animal triad of Hod-Tiferet-Nezah it can dominate and cut a path through the mass of vegetable humanity. This phenomenon is seen in business, the sciences and art, and in government. Such animal individuals live out their lives with a sense of speciality. They are different, and self-important enough to override lesser folk, use them, and manipulate them for their own ambition, be it for self-aggrandizement or in apparent idealism. A sense of identity is very strong in people working off the Hod-Tiferet-Nezeh triad. They can see what others cannot. They are awake in relation to ordinary people. Moreover, they possess the will to have their way and if necessary defeat any other animal man or woman who opposes them. History is full of the conflicts of such people, using lesser-willed beings to serve their purposes. However, it is not at all as they imagine it. Larger celestial forces in fact use them to fulfil a cosmic plan. A great upheaval such as the fall of the Roman Empire or the First World War are examples.

The First World War was the flash-point of a long cosmic-terrestrial pressure that had been building up in Europe. Historically there had been very little major political movement within the structure of European society since the French Revolution, despite several abortive attempts at reform. However, the continent had in fact undergone, because of the highly creative period of the Industrial Revolution, considerable economic and social change, and this had brought about a deep strain within the European international community. It manifested externally in alliances and tensions between the national groupings of the central European powers, the West and Russia. It was seen in the military and naval jockeying for power between Germany, Britian and France, which feared the German army and wished to avenge her defeat of 1871. Meanwhile, internally, throughout the Austro-Hungarian and Russian empires there were powerful political currents pressuring the Establishment while the same cosmic screw turning precipitated subject people's risings in the Balkans and in Ireland. Outwardly there was a stable peace, but anyone with insight sensed the mounting tension. In Kabbalistic terms, millions of Yeziratic bodies were receiving an active influx of stimulus from the celestial world. Positively, this same influence had brought about a period of great invention and discovery in science, and several important movements in the arts, as well as the already-mentioned impulse of mass emigration overseas. The negative aspect was manifested in political and industrial unrest and in the enormous investment in men and material for war. The build-up took many years to accumulate under the fixed regime of an early nineteenth-century concept of government which held millions in social and economic bondage while concentrating power and wealth in the hands of a hereditary elite. The head of steam, by August 1914, was ready to burst when the sun in Leo was in opposition to Uranus and Jupiter, and Saturn and Mars were square to each other. A formidable and explosive mixture in the macrocosm as the Yeziratic Tiferet brought a strained Hokhmah and Hesed, and a mutually frustrating Binah and Gevurah into maximum tension both above and below, without and within.

Thus it was, as individual animal people all around Europe struggled with each other, driven by personal ambition, fused into opposing camps, then alliances, as national groupings sought to hold or gain ascendancy while simultaneously keeping the now stirring continental mass of ordinary folk in their economic and social places. Seen in detail, the fates of individuals interwoven over the years had brought about a particular flavour in the establishments of each nation. The similarities and differences between the British and German navies is an example. This in turn determined the way in which alignments were made and broken. By the summer of 1914, an international situation had developed in which it only needed one incident to trigger a giant release of psychological and physical (or Yeziratic and Asiyyatic) Force and Form. It happened when the fate of an animal man of peasant stock crossed the fate of (probably) a vegetable man of royal birth to create a moment of destiny. As Gavrilo Princip shot Archduke Ferdinand, heir to the Austrian throne, on a summer day (when the moon-ego and Mars-judgement were conjunct), in an obscure town called Sarajevo, the lives of millions of people began to be changed. Within weeks there was a war madness everywhere, with men rushing to die for causes that had no real meaning to them as individuals. Animal men and vegetable men were swept into four years of violence and brutality that removed any claim that Europe had to represent a centre of civilization. The conflict spread round the globe, and essentially non-European empires such as the Ottoman Empire, that had been stable for many centuries, collapsed while great new nations like America broke their century-old isolationist doctrines to become involved in the general conflict. By the end of the War the political and social face of humanity had radically altered. The process of change that had been started by Princip's shot still continues to this day, the Second World War and its consequent political, scientific and social revolutions bear witness.

From the point of view of our study, the fate of animal individuals is merely a silver thread among the myriads of copper threads of ordinary people. This reminds us of the *Pargod* or Curtain of Souls that hangs before the Throne of God. Here we see, in a generation, the interweaving of many destinies, each one related to those above and below and to each side. Taking the analogue as a precise image of the human situation, it can be seen how the thread of a soul can touch many others, some near and some far, and some so closely bound that fatal connections can occur. Seen in terms of group connection, this phenomenon is observed in the fates of families, communities and even nations. Moreover, the thread of destiny that passes through the skein of fate is sometimes clearly revealed when an individual either unconsciously becomes the focus of an epoch, as Napoleon did, or changes the course of history by a conscious act, as Joshua ben Miriam of Nazareth did. However, such important turning points in the life of mankind are contingent upon the presence of everyone concerned, so that, from the viewpoint of destiny or Beriah, no life is irrelevant, not even that of the most lowly beggar in Jerusalem who was miraculously cured, or the meanest French soldier who maliciously shot Russian peasants as Moscow burned. All have their impersonal parts to play in a grand unfolding cosmic design, which it takes a very long and deep view of the Universe to perceive. Such a vision is not acceptable to people living exclusively in the World of Yezirah, who only recognize the passing ego-Yesodic view of life as reality.

Beyond the bio-psychology of the Keter of the physical body lies the upper and inner part of the psyche. Here, in this invisible world of the unconscious, are Yeziratic and Beriatic influences at work which go largely unnoticed by natural man. This is because at such a level the influences of the superior planets, that is, those outside the Earth's orbit (as opposed to the inferior, of the moon, Mercury and Venus), and the Galaxy have a longer and more subtle effect on mankind. For the natural man such influences are very general, but for the truly individual the changes in this upper and inner part of the psyche are very specific. Here begins fate in the particular, which is the instrument of destiny.

20. *Fate: Particular*

So far we have only touched on what is sometimes called the natural law of large numbers. Under this general law, the vegetable and animal people of the lower Face of Yezirah act as the upper Earth to the lower Earth of the vegetable and animal kingdoms. In this capacity, they perform as terrestrial humanity, more or less earth-bound and subject to the Wheel of Life and Death. However, there are other levels in mankind who, although they too are born, walk the earth and die, are not entirely ruled by the laws of nature. These people are those who have worked for and acquired real individualities. Such people have a distinct as against a general fate.

What is fate? Fate is the line of development in a single life-time that follows a particular set of characteristics. It may be ascending or descending, good or bad; its aim can be clear or obscure to the person living it or people observing it, but it is never without a pattern. Fate, operating as the tool of destiny, always fits into the grand design of the many other lives existing at the same time. Moreover, it relates directly or indirectly to those who have been before and will be after the fate has been completed. Each fate or life is specially designed for that stage in the person's total existence of lives, so that that brief span of years is a specific moment in the cosmic drama, in which it is a vital thread in the weave of humanity's destiny.

Fate is the Yeziratic expression, life by life, of a human destiny which was originally created in Beriah. When a human being is sent down into Yezirah as a pure and virgin spirit, it is given a soul to enclothe it. There in the Treasure House of Souls it is held until, tradition tells us, it is called to be incarnated into a physical body. This occurs when a situation arises that precisely suits the needs of that spirit's purpose, and so the soul-encrusted spirit is born into a physical body and into a particular family, time and place. At the moment of birth, the Yeziratic Tree of the soul's psychological body is set according to the state of the macrocosmic World at that moment. This gives a particular setting of Yeziratic Sefirot, in that the position of the sun, moon and planets in the Zodiac and in relationship to each other and the Earth determines the psychological configuration peculiar to that person alone.

How does this influence that individual's fate? The answer might be perceived in the examination of an actual life. Napoleon Bonaparte was born in the year 1769, when Uranus was in Taurus, Neptune in Virgo and Saturn in Cancer. These slow-moving planets created the outer and inner psychological background to a particular generation of children born around that time. However, in more local focus, in the month of August, Jupiter and Mars were in Scorpio and Virgo respectively, while the sun was in Leo. On the 15th of the month Venus was in seven degrees of Cancer and Mercury in six of Leo, while the fastest moving celestial body, the moon, at Napoleon's actual moment of birth was in twenty-eight degrees of Capricorn. All these celestial positions were fixed exactly to the minute of a degree as the seventh degree of Libra came up over the horizon of the Bonaparte house in Ajaccio on the island of Corsica. This gave the baby a unique moment in time to enter the World. No other person, unless they were born in the same bed within the same four minutes as Napoleon, could have the identical psycho-biological crystallization.

All those born at about that period were products and children of that specific time. When the older generation eventually left the world-stage to Napoleon's generation, the situation was already building up for the historical drama in which he would play so prominent a part. Without the general background of revolution sweeping France and indeed threatening all Europe, Napoleon could never have risen to be what he had inherent in him. The macrocosm generated in the microcosm of humanity an atmosphere of social unrest and political idealism. Napoleon was drawn into one local storm centre by his particular psychology and its gifts, and by the French nation's need for its political vacuum to be filled by a leader of his calibre and temperament. Others tried to fill the eye of the tempest, but they failed because they could not hold the focus of the swirling mass and mood of the French people. At first, it was Napoleon's charismatic temperament that brought him into notice; later this quality grew to fascinate the public, then dominate and integrate the turbulent political factions into a unity, so that there was eventually a national recognition of the identity of his individual fate and the destiny of France. This marriage of the man and the nation was to precipitate a large international drama, in which the rise and fall of the Napoleonic era was to affect a whole generation of Europeans living at that time.

The individual mechanism behind Napoleon's fate is the juxtaposition of emphasis in his Yeziratic Tree. Napoleon had a Leonine Tiferet and a Capricornian Yesod; that is, he possessed a Self that operated through the simultaneous Keter of the physical Tree as a dominating will over the other animal men as well as the vegetable masses, whom he skilfully organized with his Capricornian ego. Both these Zodiacal signs are preoccupied with power. Leo seeks dominion through the Self, and Capricorn seeks to rule through law. Both of these qualities were characteristic of Napoleon's psychology. The presence of Mars in Virgo gave Napoleon's Gevurah a practical precision and Jupiter in Scorpio a focused Hesedic or deep emotional driving power and charisma, which made people both fear and love him. This was generated by the fact that the two planets of psychological Judgement and Mercy were well aspected to each other, which meant a free flow of emotional power and direction. The reverse occurs between Saturn and the moon, which are in opposition, and thus the Yesodic ego and the understanding of Binah, being often opposed, are subject to error. This, plus the fact that Napoleon had Saturn close to the meridian and in the House of worldly achievement and ambition, brought about the Emperor's downfall through ego's misunderstanding of the military and political fact that all Europe would eventually go against him.

While the above technical account is obviously very brief, it gives us a glimpse of the particular crystallization of a psyche. Thus we see how one Sefirah is over-emphasized or repressed, or is in conflict with another. This creates a complex situation in the psyche, generating strengths and weaknesses, talents, ineptitudes and emotional and intellectual blocks and easy passages. Such a configuration of psychological principles focuses into what appears to be a single nature which we recognize in ourselves or in others. This in turn makes us drawn to or repelled by different circumstances, and so we select and attract a particular kind of life. This life might be inclined towards science or the arts or, as in Napoleon's case, the pursuit of power and glory. Thus, as we progress through our life, our fate, if we act as individuals who are not swayed by the things that rule most people, becomes more and more apparent. Moreover, because we are as we are, with all our gifts and foibles, we seek those like us for friends and professional colleagues. In a like manner we have love relationships with those who either complement or meet the needs generated by the particular balance of Sefirot in our psychology. This fated type of relationship is quite distinct from the connections of the body. Physical relationships as such are of Asiyyah, and may be no more than practical business connections or affairs of passion. Any fated Yeziratic meeting is concerned with the psyche and often the unconscious part at that.

The unconscious aspect of the psyche operates beyond the threshold of the Yeziratic Hod-Nezah line. Thus, the promptings and motivations of the superior planets and their effects of the upper and inner Sefirot are often never noticed, except in moments of illumination or crisis. Such events, again, are usually fatal and change the mechanical course of a life. They usually occur when a configuration of forces both planetary and psychological bring to a head a problem or a fruition of work that has long been in the making. Most people do not have these major crises .They never take the risk to be individuals, no matter how much they protest that they are. As ego- or Yesod-orientated folk they are

only affected in a big way when external mundane events over-
take them, like the decline of an industry or the outbreak of a war.
This does not mean to say that they do not suffer, learn and grow,
but that the process is gradual and natural, and it may take many
lifetimes to learn one lesson. The person who chooses to be an
individual accelerates his evolution, and this brings a greater testing of the spirit embodied in the Yeziratic anatomy of the soul.

The difference between the self-chosen individual and the mass
of humanity is that the individual lives according to all his
Yeziratic Tree, whereas the purely natural person lives only
according to the lower psychological Face and the body Tree.
Moreover, this difference is sometimes greater than one individual
going his own fatal way because, being directly influenced by
the upper part of Yezirah, the presence and criteria of yet another
World, that of Beriah, is occasionally involved. Our example of
Napoleon illustrates the point. While such a man might be seen
as a minor dictator dominating, for a few years, the lower Worlds,
he also served the upper realm of Creation, although in his case as
an unconscious tool of destiny. Thus, while he lived out his personal fate, he also performed the cosmic task of purging an ancient,
outdated political system, just as other conquerors, such as Attila
the Hun, had done. When Napoleon had served his purpose,
Fortune, or the mood of the time, took him from the scene, and
he died an isolated catalyst on a remote South Atlantic island.

Not all men of fate who become figures of destiny are so un-
aware of the grand design that moves through history. Some
actually know and monitor its course, because they operate at a
level above that of the celestial influences. This will be discussed
later, because first we must further open out the Kabbalistic
examination of fate and destiny.

21. Gilgulim: Transmigration

'Many are the Worlds through which they revolve, and each revolution is wonderous in many hidden ways, but men do not know or perceive these things.' Thus speaks the *Zohar* [III 99b] upon transmigration.

At any one time there are usually three generations of people living on the Earth. Children, parents and grandparents are roles that most human beings pass through during the course of a single life. Nature's rhythms are such that a new generation is born when the grandparents have passed their prime and are beginning to age, so that the child is brought up in the presence of all the ages of mankind. Thus the growing individual sees childhood in the family, youth in experiment, prime in fulfilment in the world and its results in middle age, and reflections on life in the old. At one point in his life he is the youngest, at another the holder of responsibility and at another the eldest, before he too faces death. Death to the natural man is the end of life because he sees nothing but an Asiyyatic corpse. The truth of the matter is different if it is viewed from the Upper Worlds.

As a soul becomes incarnated at birth so it becomes discarnated at death. In Kabbalistic terms this means that the Asiyyatic body ceases to exist as an organism and dissolves back into its elemental Force and Form, while the consciousness of the middle column is withdrawn upwards into Yezirah. Tradition states that this sets up a reverberation throughout all the Worlds, though it is not usually perceived. In the case of vegetables and animals, the consciousness retires back into the Keter of Asiyyah, there to be sent out again by the spirit of the species into the seed of another generation of that animal or plant. In the case of man, who is in fact an angelic being walking the Earth, the situation is different. He shifts dimensions from the upper Face of Asiyyah to the lower Face of Yezirah at death, where an important processing occurs before his next stage of development.

Most esoteric traditions agree, and Kabbalah is no exception, that a human being is far from dead when he dies physically. All accounts of the post mortem state report that upon the death of the body the psychological image of the person remains near the corpse for a brief period while it becomes used to the idea of death. Moreover, a process begins whereby the dead person reviews the whole of his life with every incident passing before him or her for judgement. Kabbalistically, these are all the memories stored around the Sefirot and in the triads of Yezirah, which run like an action replay film before the screen of the dead person's Yesod. Such an unreeling of the life in reverse, we are informed brings both intense pain and pleasure, as good and evil acts are relived with extraordinary clarity of detail. Nothing is missed, even those events that have been repressed or long forgotten are screened for the person to see and judge as a performace of his life. Hints of this process are observed in old people approaching death and even in the young who come close to death during some illness or accident. The recurring phenomenon of seeing the whole of one's life unfold before one while drowning or falling is not uncommon and strengthens the evidence that this process is begun when the physical body is begining to separate from the psychological body in anticipation of death.

Kabbalistic tradition says that after this unfolding of the life has been completed a post mortem period of cleansing or purgatory is gone through. This again occurs in Yezirah, where all the imbalances and imperfections are stored during life. The process is said to vary between the difficult and the extremely painful, depending on how much and how many laws have been transgressed. The result of this purification that takes place primarily in the soul triad of Gevurah-Tiferet-Hesed is that initial Judgement and Mercy are executed by the individuals on themselves, and so they rise into the Heaven of Beriah, stay where they are in the Paradise or Purgatory of Yezirah, descend into the flesh again in Asiyyah, or go down into the Gehinnom of Hell. All these symbols of Heaven, Paradise, Purgatory and Hell are allegories of states of being most people have already experienced in life.

If they rise to enter the Kingdom of Heaven, they have usually either completed a long cycle of lives in which there has been a slow evolution or they have attained, by conscious effort, a rapid ascension during a few lifetimes or one extraordinary lifetime. This is possible by great and deep work on self-perfection, or by virtue of the fact that they were already well-evolved spiritual beings. This brings up the point that humanity may again be divided into three types: the first two are people who incline to the left and right pillars and are drawn to perform during one or many lifetimes the functional roles of being either upholders of Form or the initiators of Force in the World. Thus we have the conservers and the radicals in every society. Some, for example, act as the communicators and teachers of Hod, others as judges and soldiers in Gevurah and some as philosophers and in government in Binah on the left column, while the professions and roles of the right might include the farmers and entertainers of Nezah, religious professionals and artists of Hesed, and prophets and revolutionaries of Hokhmah. People of the central column are quite different. They are concerned not with maintaining the world but with bringing the upper levels down into it, that is why such people on death may return to the Heaven from whence they came by choice in the first place, having in previous lives perfected themselves to a degree in the Knowledge of the purpose of Existence.

People who pause where they are after death, we are told, find one of the seven Yeziratic levels most appropriate to their being. Here, in the joyful and dreadful zones of Paradise and Purgatory, where the rewards and punishments of life are experienced, time, tradition tells us, is quite different from that which operated on Earth, and so is the way people exist. In this state of pure Yezirah, the myriad facets and essence of an individual are held in all their forms, and so there is no fixed and solid image; also, here are gathered all the connections with other souls, living and dead, who are part of its fatal group, which in turn fits into the grand destiny that the Providence of Beriah is slowly unfolding throughout created Space and Time. Thus, one individual may not incarnate for long terrestrial periods, but have to wait or work in the Yeziratic levels of Purgatory and Paradise until the right conditions below in Asiyyah have matured which will suit his evolution and the cosmic purpose of Heaven. Then he is sent down, perhaps to be born along with souls from the same group at a similar time, but perhaps in different families or thousands of miles away. Nevertheless, on a fatal meeting these souls recognize each other, although the reason why may not be manifest until certain general and individual events have been accomplished. If they are not, then the operation may have to be repeated again sooner or later in another place at another time.

For those who return to be reborn almost immediately the Kabbalistic term 'Gilgulim', the 'Wheels' or the 'Revolutions', has a strong meaning. It originates from a Biblical phrase in I Samuel 25:29 about lives being whirled round like a stone and then thrown out of a sling back into life. This occurs when a person cannot face the next World and its purifying processes and so he or she seeks a quick rebirth to avoid any spiritual responsibility. As it happens, no one can escape cosmic or psychological law, and so they are simply reborn into a physical situation that precisely meets in punishment and reward their spiritual need. Sometimes it is not at all pleasant, so that, we are told, the criminal finds himself in a position where he is stolen from and the cruel woman becomes the recipient of hate; it is likewise for the good, but in contrast, whose situation can be increasingly interesting, so that over a series of lives the soul gradually works on its perfection through a sequence of fatal situations and relationships that act as a physical Paradise and Purgatory (purification is not always a painful or suffering process). These slowly evolving people live in the lower Face of Yezirah or the state of upper Earth, and may be easily recognized by their quality of light despite the sometimes strangely difficult circumstances they appear to be in. Providence does not always work through the easy and obvious. We get what we need, not what we want, from life – whose object is to evolve the individual and unfold the Divine plan.

This cosmic purpose is even carried out in the Hell of Gehinnom, which is a symbol for that place where that which is corrupt or perverse is melted down for reformation or eventually disintegrated back into its pure elements again. Now it is said that there are seven levels in the Tree of Hell and that these are divided into two Faces of impurity. The upper 'Palaces of Filth', as they are called, are the places where those who have committed redeemable sins reside. This means that they have not lost the possibility of rescue if they can dissolve the block or bent function that brought them to the state of Hell. An example of this may be seen in the criminal who knows he is breaking the law but nevertheless will carry on as long as he can get away with it. Life after life, he lives most of his physical existence in jail, until he suddenly sees that it is only taking him deeper down into Hell and further away perhaps from his wife and children and ordinary humanity. With such a reform, however slight, the movement upwards begins, and he can eventually, if he is constant, enter the World of General Evolution again and even attempt the Gates of Heaven, which more than one criminal turned saint has succeeded in opening. This upper Hell would correspond to the bottom Face of Asiyyah.

The Lower Hell, or true Gehinnom beyond the Malkhut of Asiyyah, is the confine of those beings who care for no one but themselves, whose own will is paramount and whose desire must be fulfilled no matter what the cost to anyone else or to the Universe. They are their own god and the World revolves about them. This is an illusion, and so real life retires from them as they reject it. So it is that they become criminally mad and totally obsessed with an unreal creation which only they inhabit. As long as they choose to inhabit this private universe they are locked in Hell No one can release them, except God, who allows them the whole of one great cosmic cycle to get out of their self-made predicament before he releases them with all the other created beings in the Jubilee of that Shemittah at the End of Days. They are the truly 'dead' and 'damned', because they are outside general creation and evolution. This is the Pit.

The cycle of life and death operates in sequence, and so most souls are repeatedly returned to live on Earth in order to gain experience that cannot be had at the level of pure Yezirah. This is because the creative tension between the angelic body of the psyche and the physical situation found on Earth can make possible things impossible in the non-material Worlds above. In basic Kabbalistic terms, in Asiyyah the realm of action, the free will of incarnate mankind, can implement events which affect the macrocosm in a way that no Spirit or Angel can, despite their power and influence in the upper Worlds. This is done in general evolution through the Gilgulim in the continuous transmigration of the human soul through many bodies and many different kinds of fate over the millennia. Thus, through the chain of a myriad lives, the spirit of Adam slowly manifests at the physical level of the Universe. The process is magnified a millionfold by the ever-expanding population of the Earth, as more and more souls are incarnated into the flesh to help Asiyyah realize, through mankind's image of its Maker, the Immanence of God.

22. Providence and Free Will

By now it must be apparent that there are two important factors at work in the life of mankind. One is Providence and the other free will. Beginning with the first, it would seem that nothing is totally accidental, no event arises without relevance, cause or purpose because of the scheme of Providence.

All things begin in the Keter of Azilut. Here is the I AM of all that was, is and shall be. From this Crown of Emanation flows the World of Perfection with all the Laws that are the model and instrument for Divine Will. Out of the eternal World of Emanation, with its ever-watching Eye of God, all things are created. Here they come under the Beriatic supervision of Heaven, from where they are sent forth into different forms in Yezirah before they are manifested physically in the material Universe of Asiyyah. All that has come into being from the Crown of Existence to the emptiness beyond the waves and particles that compose the atom, is sustained by the Will of the Absolute, that it might complete its purpose so that God should see God.

In order that this objective might be fulfilled, the Divine Will provides everything in existence with what it needs at the correct time and place. Nothing occurs outside the great order that is unfolding within the cosmic cycle. However, there are two levels of operation or Providence at work within the Universe, one being general and the other individual. The reason for this is that while most of the Universe is fixed by the laws of its Worlds and their inhabitants, there is one creature who possesses free will. Such a gift grants the power to change levels and accelerate the cosmic processes or even reverse them, should the entity wish to go against God's Will. This creature is the human being.

Mankind, as we have seen, is a species unto itself. Unlike all other creatures, which are confined to either the upper or lower Worlds, mankind can spread itself to the top or bottom of the Jacob's Ladder of existence. As a Beriatic spirit, a Yeziratic soul and an Asiyyatic body, mankind is unusual enough, but its real uniqueness lies in that it possesses free will as a legacy from its ancestors Adam and Eve, who were made in the image of their Creator. However, the full prerogative, it must be stressed, is not exercised by mankind as a whole, because most choose to remain under the general laws of Providence.

General Providence is well illustrated by the ecological ladder of Nature. We have seen how the galaxy of the Milky Way, its stars, the sun, the planets and the moon have produced the physical theatre for organic life on Earth. It has also been shown how each species arrives and departs according to the needs of the Earth and Nature. Looking in greater detail, the ecological pyramid of any given time is a very delicately balanced structure, with each species of plant and animal supporting or being supported by the rest. This is General Providence. Thus, the hawk lives on smaller birds which exist on insects which eat plants, and so on. However, within this precise arrangement is a broad margin of latitude, in that a hawk may kill this or that bird and the bird eat that or this insect. The individual does not count, only the species, and so while the mean level of, say, grasshoppers is maintained within a seasonal rhythm, the fate of individual grasshoppers is under the law of large numbers. Such a random fortune occurs throughout nature and also applies to those members of incarnate mankind who choose to live at the vegetable and animal levels of humanity.

People living under General Providence operate just from the Asiyyatic Tree and the lower Face of Yezirah. Their lives, if they exist only to eat and procreate, are based on the external world, which like the vegetable kingdom around them is subject to the seasons and to periods of glut and dearth. Nothing particularly dramatic happens as the round of lives passes through generations of ordinary and average country or town folk. Nor indeed do many want drama, but only wish to be left alone to live. Taken further, it may be said, for example, that the same group of souls reincarnate in the same village over the centuries so that they take on a leap-frogging pattern of rebirths and a repeated cycle of child, parent and grandparent within, say, the family that has perhaps farmed the same land in Buckinghamshire, England, for five hundred years (sometimes old family portraits look remarkably like the present family). The only thing that ever disturbs the rhythm of vegetating lives is when the more sensitive animal part of mankind, responding to cosmic change, precipitates revolutions in the greater society of which the village is part and which it supports with its work. This might cause some of the sons and daughters, as in time of war, to travel and enter the animal level of mankind. On returning they might attempt to alter the pattern of their elders, but the shock wave soon fades and they either leave for the bigger world or become, in time, village elders themselves and maintain the old ways of a quiet rhythmic life. In such a situation, General Providence takes care of the community but is not concerned with the nonconformist or the individual, who must seek either a place in the animal level of mankind or higher still.

Two important points must be made concerning vegetable communities before we leave the subject of General Providence, and they are that the right of individual choice is never denied, and that Providence always creates opportunities for people to escape the general laws which operate at this level. An actual historical event will illustrate how Providence works negatively and positively for those who choose to be individuals. A certain dictator let it be known that he had had a dream that he must get rid of all the aliens in his country so that only native nationals could run the economy. Those aliens who agreed with the President that the omen was from Heaven, but for different reasons, immediately left with family and fortune. Later a government edict was issued that required those who remained to become nationals of that country or remain aliens. In due time the technically foreign aliens, many of whose families had lived in the country for decades, were deported without their hard-earned fortunes. This seemed at the time tragic, but it was soon considered a blessing to have got out of the country alive when the remaining naturalized aliens also lost their businesses and in some cases their lives. The significance of the story from the point of view of our study is that Providence actually warned, through the instrument of the dictator himself, that a situation was generating in which there were several options. Those who could see beyond the vegetable comforts chose to get out, whether earlier or later, while those who in effect did not choose to see what would inevitably happen were caught up in the law which governs vegetable humanity when one community begins to expand and take over the ground, root and sustenance of another. Such events might appear a cruel kind of Providence, but there is always the factor of choice. If it is not exercised, individual Providence, which is mankind's privilege, is lost.

A person who lives at the human animal level is still under the General Providence. His or her life has more individuality, but this is only relative to the millions who live vegetable and routine lives. Such an individual might fight to the top of a profession and be its leader as a pop singer or surgeon, but he will in effect be only filling a throne that must be sat on by one animal individual or another (a person of destiny is quite a different matter). According to the animal man's talents and stamina, his kingship is held only until someone younger, more gifted or experienced, or just with something new, usurps his position. Under the law of General Providence, he will find all the support he needs as long as he fulfils the current requirements of the community he serves, be it a military junta, a board of directors or a mob of gangsters. He is still subject to accident; that is, external factors that can bring him into prominence or unseat him from the throne. Here too choice and individual Providence are possible, but because of the animal desire to dominate free will is lost in the compulsion of the urge to win.

To gain an insight into how General and individual Providence might work, let us take a look at your life. You were born of specific parents and brought up in a particular way. During the childhood period you probably lived within a general vegetable rhythm, with most of your physical and psychological needs being met. On puberty, you began to assert your independence, just like millions of other adolescents, and compete and participate in the love game between the sexes. Then you went to college or work, where you were confronted with your first real decision in being an adult, in that you had to commit yourself to some direction in life. This is the point when a person can come out of the general law into that of individual Providence. As you will have no doubt noticed, most people opt for one of the two levels of the lower Yeziratic Face: they either enter the rhythmic cycle of producing goods or services for the community as they pass through their life of growth, reproduction, decay and death, or they seek leadership of whatever field they have chosen. Few actually choose to be individuals, instead of living according to the pressures of the society they find themselves in. All will protest that they are individuals, but the facts, alas, prove different. Often even the most radical people are conformist radicals of that generation. Individuality is much deeper than the mask of fashionable originality.

Real individuality was present right at the beginning of your existence when your virgin spirit was created. At this point, your character and purpose were determined so that you might aid in the grand design. On descent into the soul, the special talents gifted to you were set out in the psyche of your Yeziratic anatomy, so that when you were incarnated you could fulfil the fate of this life and your long-term cosmic destiny. However, because free will exists, you or anyone else may choose to ignore or forget your talents and task, that is your individuality, and so bury yourself in physical reality. Such a moment comes, not at birth when most of the memory of the upper Worlds is obliterated by the shock of being incarnated, but at the inception of adulthood. All young people, especially from puberty onwards, question the meaning of life, if only just for the once, as perhaps they suddenly notice the stars or experience the death of someone they know. The result of their choice, whether or not to live according to their inherent spirit, determines not only this but often subsequent lives. Thus, someone who chooses to ignore his gifts, and the job he is meant to do, stifles his individuality beneath the law of General Providence – although the person might receive the grace of luck.

Luck is being in the right place at the right time. Here again general and individual Providence operate. The former is under the law of random events, as when a person hopes, but is surprised to win a sweepstake. Often, such people are totally unprepared for the event, and their new-found wealth destroys the pattern that held their lives together. For example, although they try to keep their old friends, there is an ever-widening rift of life-style, and so good luck, turns into rich ill-fortune. This is the result of general as against individual luck.

Individual luck is not really luck but the fruit of perhaps many lifetimes. An individual may have been a villain or a hero, a wise man or a fool, but in each life the circumstances he is born into are precisely placed and timed so that he should meet certain people or events. This is otherwise known as fate, although good or ill luck often appears to come out of the blue. Such happenings present a moment of choice that will take one towards or away from one's true nature. Apparent ill luck may be a blessing in disguise; and so individual Providence takes care to save a man from real harm, or to bring him closer into contact with the task for which he was born by placing in his way people or events that exactly coincide with his need at the time.

Again, let us look at your own situation. You are reading this book. What brought you to this point is not only the myriads of small and great events that have made up your life, and the several thousand people who have influenced you, but the result of perhaps many previous lives that have made you gradually remember where you came from. I know this because you would not be reading this kind of book if you were not. The point is now, as always, what do you choose? Do you totally reject, partially accept or seriously consider these ideas as making some sense of the Universe you are now living in? The choice is yours because you possess the gift of free will.

The concept of free will is frequently misunderstood. In the context of total existence, the exercise of choice is limited to the level of the particular time the individual finds himself in. Thus, one can change a given situation only moment by moment, in relation to oneself, because everything about one is under the general laws that make the Universe work as a whole. Take, for example, a conscript soldier in battle. After a sedentary lifetime, or perhaps many lives, in a small town where he did not ever consider anything too deeply, he is confronted by the thought of his own violent death and that of other men whom he must kill. The realization may shock him out of the vegetable state, through the animal attitude of pure survival in the lower Yeziratic Tree, and into the triad of the soul and conscience. Such a moment changes his life, or even future lifetimes, if, despite his death, he perceives that a man must not live and die like a plant or animal. This kind of event will alter the balance of the Universe, but only to the degree of that private soldier's capability. For someone working at a higher level, the possibility of affecting events is greater, although it must be observed that even such a great man as Socrates had his free will prescribed within limits. He chose to accept his execution for influencing society even though he was offered escape, because to have avoided the sentence of the court would have invalidated his belief in obedience to the rule of law. Because of his free choice, his action made real his philosophy, which has profoundly affected Western thought.

The above examples of how free will is confined to specific instances explain the paradox that God knows all that will happen yet does not interfere with human choice. They also indicate how a human being can choose to deny his individuality or truth, although, sooner or later, he must inevitably choose, of his own free will, to remain dormant or submit to the Way of Heaven. This means in Kabbalistic terms that he moves out of the vegetable and animal security of the lower Face of the psyche and into the triad of the soul which hovers above the body and between the Trees of Earth and Heaven.

Once a person has placed his centre of gravity in the Yeziratic triad of Gevurah-Tiferet-Hesed, the quality of his life changes radically, as he comes under a morality that has little or no

relevance to the social codes of the Natural World. Outwardly
his fellows may note little alteration in his being, but inwardly
he will perceive that with choice he has the very real capability of
increasing the presence of good and evil in the World. Such a
responsibility is not natural, but then neither is the spiritual power
by which his existence is now governed. He is in effect preparing
to re-enter Eden and consciously participate in the Worlds of the
Soul and Spirit while he lives in the flesh. Such an occupation
demands great skill and knowledge, and individual Providence
usually provides a fated and vital contact with someone who is
directly involved in the Work of the supernatural Worlds. In
every spiritual tradition there are always teachers ready to instruct,
but they are never perceived until the disciple selects himself as a
candidate for receiving instruction. This phenomenon is the essential relationship between individual Providence and free will.
When the connection is made, the lower and the upper Worlds
are no longer separate in that person. All begins to fuse into one,
as the Workings of Heaven perceived as Objective Knowledge
grant an insight into the realm of the supernatural that underlies
the phenomena of the Natural World.

23. The Supernatural

There are basically two kinds of knowledge: Natural and Supernatural. The first is acquired by living in this World and the second by remembering, or being taught, about the next World and beyond. As regards the first, this is life in the flesh and its basic lessons cannot be ignored if only to survive in the human vegetable condition. But life is, as one great Kabbalist said, more than eating and drinking; it is a particular epoch in the itinerary of the spirit's progression down from the upper Worlds, through materiality and back again. The sojourn in the exile of physical life may be long or short depending on the use of free choice or the task assigned to that particular spirit. Most spirits shuttle to and fro between the Worlds of Yezirah and Asiyyah, as the Yeziratic vehicle of the soul inhabits body after body in a chronological line of lives that rise and fall according to the performance of that particular Self. In this way there is a general evolution or reintegration into, or disintegration out of, the cosmic scheme. However, there are some human entities who do not perform as general factors in evolution on the side pillars of function, but act through the central column of Knowledge.

The difference between those who maintain the world, through the functions of fear and love, and those who work from Knowledge is that the people who operate off the central column take on the responsibility for themselves. Those who work off the outer columns may be great or humble, roadsweepers, archbishops, scientists or even prophets, but they may not necessarily know what they really are and why they are there. The person of the central column is one who knows what he is doing and where he is. In Kabbalah, like many other traditions, such individuals are called 'those who know the secret'.

Now, the secret is open. There is no exclusion. Nor has there ever been, despite the attempts of corrupted priest craft to make it exclusive. It was never exclusive, except in that a person may exclude himself by his refusal to be what he is and to see what his individual and cosmic purpose may be. Here again is free will. Thus, a person himself chooses to be initiated into the Way of Knowledge.

Tradition tells us that everyone is born with Knowledge inherent in them, and indeed Socrates demonstrated to his sophisticated disciples that even a simple peasant knew a great deal about cosmic law if he was asked the right questions. Kabbalah states that the Knowledge is present in man because a human being contains all the Worlds and the Divine laws that govern them. Moreover, an individual has access to this Knowledge in three ways. However, before we come to these, let us look at the Knowledge of the supernatural Worlds from a mythological and historical point of view.

Legend informs us that God personally instructed the senior Archangels in the nature and purpose of the Universe, and that one of these Great Spirits, Raziel, whose name means 'Secret of God', appeared to Adam three days after he had been expelled from Eden. Now Raziel is the Archangel of Hokhmah or Wisdom, and his revelation was recorded in a 'book' that was handed down over the generations of mankind to those who wished to know about the World and its purpose. Tradition says that it passed through Noah's hands and came to Abraham. From him it was handed, via Jacob, down to Levi, from whose tribe Moses came. It was then given to the Elders of Israel, who kept it intact within the accumulating outer Tradition of Judaism. Such a body of knowledge cannot be written down, because it is essentially a matter of the spirit; and so, despite the vast literature, to which the present book is an addition, Kabbalah or 'Receiving' remains an essentially oral connection between the generations of seekers and teachers of Truth. This story applies equally to all living spiritual traditions.

Looking at the line of Knowledge historically, one may guess that mankind acquired insight into the supernatural Worlds in two ways. In the first, some early people either dimly recalled where they had originally come from, and worked to regain entrance to the next World, or they were indirectly or directly instructed by beings from above. Historical evidence and observation of today's primitive peoples indicates that there are always some who are particularly interested in things not of this world. Their reasons may be to gain status over their physically stronger peers as witch doctors, or because of a genuine fascination with the unseen; either way, they appear to acquire powers to perceive or control natural and elemental entities that ordinary people sense but cannot see. This is the psychic faculty of the lower Yeziratic Face, which as the upper Face of Asiyyah can detect and control, if there is enough Will, the zone where natural and psychological Force and Form meet. Thus a shaman or sorcerer can, over a long period of mental discipline, or through repeated lives, acquire the gift to enter the World of Formation and manipulate Asiyyah from the lowest part of the next World. This sorcery is a dangerous practice because it is not related to upper Yezirah. At such a point a teacher is needed.

Among early men, an instructor would come in an internal or external form. The internal would be via the upper inner Trees of the psyche and spirit, while an outer manifestation would be in the appearance of an angelic being. Now, while the Bible speaks of the *Benai ha*ELOHIM, the Sons of the ELOHIM, taking the daughters of mankind to wife (Genesis 6:4), Biblical legends and Kabbalistic teaching explain in greater detail the relationship of the angelic tutor to the truth-seeking human being. According to myth, Enoch, the seventh in generation from Adam, walked with God, that is lived always in his presence and went God's Way. This was in great contrast to most of the people of Enoch's time, who were eventually to be destroyed in the Flood. Enoch later appeared to Rabbi Ishmael, in Talmudic times, and told him that it was because he had been such an odd man out that he was taken up into Heaven without tasting death. There Enoch was translated, by the Fire of Azilut, into the Archangel Metatron who resides at the highest point of Heaven in the Keter of Beriah (see figure 13). Here, where the Tiferet of Emanation is, Enoch became the Created Spirit of the Presence and acted in God's Name to oversee and instruct mankind. As a man, Enoch knew the human situation. Known as Idris in the Sufi tradition, Enoch chose to remain and teach those below rather than rise and reunite totally with EN SOF.

Below the place of Enoch-Metatron, in the seventh Heaven, on the central column that carries the direct Will of God, is the Azilutic Yesod of EL HAI SHADDAI, the ALMIGHTY LIVING GOD. There is no Archangel here in this Divine Foundation, and yet Metatron is higher because he is also traditionally called the Lesser YAHVEH. Here is YAHVEH-ELOHIM, the CREATOR, seeing the Image of God at the highest created level through the man Enoch, whose name means 'Initiated' or 'Dedicated'. Now, the Yesod of Azilut is the Daat of Beriah, and from here the Knowledge of the Image of God flows directly down into the Tiferet of Beriah, watched over by the Archangel Michael, whose name it will be recalled means 'Like unto God'.

Michael stands in the place where the three upper Worlds meet, and he, from his position at the centre of Creation, watches over the Archangel Gabriel who operates at the Beriatic Yesod, the equivalent of the Daat of the psyche. From here Gabriel passes on knowledge concerning Creation to any human being who wishes to listen and who can climb out of the lower Face of Yezirah and into the Sefirah of the Self, where the lower three Worlds meet. At this place of the Self stands Sandalphon, the tallest of the Archangels in Beriah. When the name Sandalphon is seen to mean 'Co-brother', it becomes apparent that his relationship, as the Beriatic Malkhut, with Metatron at the Beriatic Keter is a special one. Indeed, they are seen in Kabbalah as a pair who sometimes fuse and manifest to incarnate human beings as Elijah the prophet, whose name means 'God is YAHVEH'.

Elijah is seen as an announcer or herald, and in Biblical myth and Kabbalistic legend he has a special place. As he, like Enoch, made a miraculous ascension into Heaven, he and Metatron are sometimes viewed as one and the same. Besides his role as the forerunner of the Messiah at the End of Days, his task is to aid those seeking guidance in spiritual matters. Thus, he appears in Islamic tradition as the strange 'Green One' who arrives then disappears at crucial moments. In Jewish folklore, he usually manifests when some miraculous help is needed. For example, before his translation he was the instrument by which fire descended from Heaven upon the drenched altar on Mount Carmel where he and God were in contest with Baal and its priests (I Kings 18). His activities after being received into Heaven on a chariot of fire (Yezirah, Beriah and Azilut) are no less extraordinary. Indeed, he appears throughout Jewish history. At one point he was a courtier to Ahasuerus at the time of Esther, in time of great national need, while at another he took a more private role to protect and instruct some individual like Rabbi Meir. Legend records that he could be anywhere in the World, at any time and in any form he chose. Once, in Roman times, we are told, this Rabbi Meir was being pursued by officials of State. When they eventually cornered him in an inn, he appeared to be in the company of a harlot, and so they passed on, thinking this could not possibly be the holy man they wanted. Elijah was the girl in this case, as he was the Arab who gave a poor but pious man two lucky coins with which to solve his money problems. Aside from the many folk stories about Elijah down the centuries, Kabbalists over the ages have asserted that Elijah had instructed them in the Teaching about Creation and the role of mankind.

The fact that Elijah is a human as well as a spiritual being is most significant, because it sets out the teaching connection up the central column from the Self to Metatron. As a human being ascends the axis of Knowledge, so he enters the seven Heavens and perceives and serves the Will of God. However, as has been noted, he does this through choice and submits gladly to the Grace that can fall upon him directly. Such a person becomes 'one who knows' and no longer reincarnates or transmigrates under the general law of development. He moves out of the rulership of random events and above the pattern of Fate, although during an incarnation he may have to pass through a particular kind of life that threads like gold through thousands of copper and silver interweaves of accident and fate that make up the fabric of one generation. Such a person may or may not come into the public eye of history, but without question he will be a person of Destiny.

The effect of such people is great; for, while an unconscious man of destiny like a Napoleon or Caesar may serve a cosmic purpose, his influence is ephemeral when compared to that of Muhammad, Buddha, Jesus or Moses. While these Sons of God are great historic figures, there are many others whose influence is felt but never seen. Such people belong to what is sometimes called the Inner Circle of Mankind. In Kabbalah, they are known as the House of Israel. It is their task to instruct those who seek the truth about themselves and their purpose in the Torah. The Hebrew word 'Torah' means literally the 'Teaching'. This body of knowledge, which is present in all living traditions, is the objective set of Laws that governs mankind and the Universe and their relationship with God. Such is the Teaching handed down from above to below by the ones who know the highest and the lowest of the Worlds. It is at this level that all true religions dissolve in their Yeziratic Form and merge into a spiritual oneness in Beriah just beneath the Divine World of Eternal perfection.

24. Torah: the Teaching

The Ultimate Truth regarding God, the World and Man must be objective. However, this can only be seen to be so when it is perceived from the absolute point of view of God. As beings in existence, created beings subject to time and separation from the Divine World of Azilut, human individuals, both incarnate and discarnate, can see the Truth only in relative terms. Therefore, the objective Teaching is handed down by Grace for instruction. At the level of the virgin spirits of the yet unborn and untried, the Universe is perceived in naïve purity; below, to the majority of the incarnate who circle through the Gilgulim of natural life and death, the World seems a very physical place. Those who have experienced life in all three lower Worlds, and have returned to the upper Face of Beriah, have perhaps the most objective view of the Cosmos. These tested and refined Spirits, no longer incarnate, instruct in the Teaching those just below in the upper Face of Yezirah, which operates as the inner circle of incarnate mankind.

As will be seen on the Extended Tree, the lower Face of Creation underlies the upper Face of Formation. This means that the World of the Spirit lies immediately behind the profoundest part of the human psyche. Thus, the Beriatic Hod and Nezah, represented by Raphael the Healer of God and Haniel the Grace of God, teach mankind the secrets of Heaven through the outer and inner Intellect, the Yeziratic Binah and Hokhmah of the individual and collective psyche.

A person at the level of the Keter of Yezirah, it will be noted, is not only placed on the central column of direct Knowledge, but at the head of the supernal triad of the psychological World, above

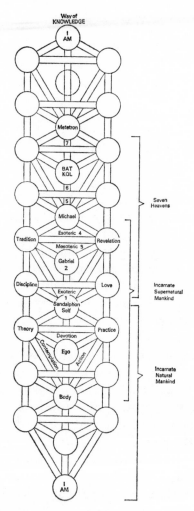

Figure 21. Way of Knowledge.   *Besides the Ways of Fear and Love of God, there is the Way of Knowledge. This approach takes the middle pillar of Consciousness and Holiness as its method. In this manner, knowledge of the body, ego and Self leads to direct instruction from those who have obtained entrance to Humanity's inner level of being. This celestial academy, as it is sometimes called, is in turn instructed by those who may or may not be incarnate or even human, although Metatron, the highest archangelic teacher, was once a man.*

Wisdom and Understanding. That person is the Anointed One or
Messiah of the era. Sometimes called the Pole of the Age, this remarkable individual may or may not be manifest to the World,
depending on the planet's need. His task is to teach all those who
have reached the esoteric or innermost level of incarnating
humanity. It is in this triad that the masters of Israel are to be found.
Israel, it must be said, is the Kabbalistic term for *everyone* of any
mystical way, who has entered the seven Heavens. Christian eso-
tericism calls them the mystical Body of Christ, and indeed every
great tradition has its equivalent name for the World of Pure
Spirit. From the point of view of this study, the esoteric triad of
living mankind contains the highest level most people can relate
to while still in the flesh. This is why the Messiah, who occupies
the Keter of Yezirah, has such an appeal.

The mesoteric or middle inner level of mankind is contained in
the Yeziratic triad of Binah-Tiferet-Hokhmah. Here, the Revelation given out by Wisdom, and the Tradition handed down by
Understanding, are transmitted down the two side functional
columns to the exoteric level or outer part of humanity, represented by the Soul triad Gevurah-Tiferet-Hesed. Here, it is passed
on down, either via the side pillars to natural humanity, as religion
or philosophy, or directly through Tiferet to individuals who
aspire to enter at the place of the Self, the Malkhut of Beriah,
known more precisely as the Kingdom of Heaven.

Now, all that has been described above applies to all true
traditions, be they great or small. The same laws must apply in
that there has to be a connection with the Axis of the Age who
oversees the people, who in turn teach, via the pillars of Love and
Fear, or Knowledge, the cosmic purpose of mankind. This operation is carried out by the Yeziratic Binah-Tiferet-Hokhmah triad,
which as the direct spiritual connection between Creation and
incarnate man implements the supervision of Heaven. The Soul
triad, as has been observed, hovers between Heaven and Earth
and constitutes the zone of free will and purification for incarnating mankind.

It is said, in many spiritual traditions, that one must die before
one is dead. This means that all the processes of Purgatory can be

passed through while an individual is still in the flesh. This is possible if a person can operate from the Soul triad, where Judgement and Mercy are exercised by the Self upon that individual in living consciousness. Normally this process occurs after death, when the vital Soul or Nefesh of the body dissolves with the dead flesh and the spirit is taken up into Beriah before being sent down again, if necessary, into the next incarnation. If the purification is accomplished before physical death, then the passage between life and death is not alarming and the person can perform a cosmic as well as an individual function. For example, many stories, ranging from the Crucifixion of Christ to the death of the Buddha and the execution of Rabbi Akiba illustrate the operation of a bigger assignment than individual attainment in relation to the Spirit. How, one might ask, does a person attain this level of being? This is where either the angelic or advanced human beings come to the aid of those below.

Over the millennia and all over the world, the same Teaching has been presented to humanity. Its forms have varied according to time and place, but the essential content and message are the same. It is found not only in all the major religions, behind the official garb, but within the depths of so-called primitive cults, which are often the remnants of a once clear body of objective knowledge. Outwardly it is carried by the orthodoxy on the two functional pillars. This can be seen in the two ways of Love and Fear of God, which hold the mass of humanity to some ethical code and encourage mankind to act with humaneness. The third way is through Knowledge, which is applied via the central column; and again all living traditions have access to this Way of Grace and Merit.

For those who wish to remain below, in the natural World, the rulership of the outer columns will shift them back and forth between expansion and contraction, or Mercy and Judgement, for as long as they choose to live under the law of General Providence. Here, they will reap the reward and punishment of their conduct and be reborn into a situation that corrects through Severity or allows them through Mercy to come closer to the middle pillar. However, for those who wish to rise above the normal earthly condition, there are many paths that lead to the Self, which is the first state of full realization. However, although the doors which open from the street of ordinary life are many, they fall into three broad categories. One person approaches by thinking, another by doing and a third by feeling. In spiritual terms these are seen as the approaches of contemplation, action and devotion. They relate to the three sub-triads that pivot on the ego of the Yeziratic Yesod.

The work that is involved in raising the level of an individual from the egocentric world of the lower Face of the psyche is long and arduous, and every tradition has techniques by which it is accomplished. These are applied through theory and practice, which are to be found at the Hod and Nezah of Yezirah. When the person has raised himself up to be capable of bringing himself, at will, into the Self, his teacher, who for a while occupies the person's Tiferet position, usually steps aside to allow the person direct access up the central column to the Sandalphon, Gabriel, Michael and Metatron levels within his own being. From here on the aspirant may not require an incarnate instructor because he can, if he raises his level of consciousness high enough, be tutored from the appropriate stage of the inner House of Mankind.

Below the level of experience here discussed, a natural man not interested in such things can have two attitudes. A positive one is to regard these matters, quite correctly, as mystical, profound and therefore beyond the natural mind. Such a one will accept the fact that some supernatural world exists, but choose to ignore it, until he has time from his worldly affairs to investigate it later. Indeed, in the Hindu tradition, the householder, having fulfilled all his worldly commitments, takes to the religous life in middle or old age so as to learn to die before dying. The negative atttitude is one of superstition. Here, ideas of the upper Worlds or glimpses of the subtle realm behind Nature often frighten and fascinate. Some people, especially those with a little experience, completely block out the unseen part of themselves and the Universe, and thereby confine themselves to a limited existence that has no rhyme or reason according to natural law: to them, the wicked appear to go unpunished and the good obtain no reward. This view is entirely self-generated, by the choice to live entirely in the flesh, which has no memory beyond its birth and dreads to contemplate its death. At worst, the attitude of the natural man to the supernatural is to use it for his own ends, so that a person who knows a little can manipulate those who know less into a state of confusion, where they cannot tell whether they should live by sensual or non-sensual criteria. That is the reason why madness is often the result of primitive or low sorcery, for the person who practises it without real knowledge or appreciation of consequences.

The imparting and receiving of knowledge flows two ways. As the being of the aspirant is raised, so the capacity to perceive and receive is increased. While many traditions advocate withdrawal from the World of Asiyyah in order to reach Beriah and go beyond, Kabbalah states that a person is born into this World for a specific reason, and that is not only to learn what he can do under difficult Earth conditions, but to bring the influx of Heaven down into the flesh and beyond into Hell if possible, so that the Divine sparks trapped in the Shell World of Kellipot may be redeemed. In this way, the cosmic level of the Universe may be raised and the Day of the final Great Redemption, when all things are in direct contact with the Divine, be brought forward. This concept has always been with the Kabbalists, who see the task of every consciously evolving human being to aid the Elyonim of the upper Worlds and to join with the Tachtonim below, so that the Heavenly influx may flow down and up through all the Worlds. The job, however, is not easy, because it requires great skill and is fraught with dangers and temptations. That is why the practical side of Kabbalah is never spoken of in detail, for it involves cosmic powers that few individuals can master unless they are of high moral calibre.*

Seen in a cosmic context, the supernatural and spiritual activities of mankind fulfil two functions. The first is to lift the human race out of the animal and vegetable stages of its evolution, and the second is to blend the upper and lower Worlds in closer harmony. This is possible because we are the only creatures that

---

*For a detailed account of the theme of this chapter, see the author's *Way of Kabbalah* (Bath, England: Gateway Books; York Beach, ME: Samuel Weiser, 1976).

can change levels within the Universe. Such a privilege gives the human race greater responsibilities than are perceived by most people living or dead, because every action, every life, indeed the whole chain of lives of every individual, affects and shifts the balance of all the created Worlds towards the left or the right, and draws the Universe away from or nearer to the Light of EN SOF. This is the gift and charge of free will which was given when the first man and woman were given the task of husbanding Eden.

25. Magic and Miracles

Because man is made in the image of God, he contains all four Worlds, and because he has free will he can, unlike any other creature, ascend or descend in them. This possibility gives a human being the potential to operate in any World and manipulate its powers and this is the basis of magic and miracles. However, such an event is not easy to accomplish, for while a human being contains a body in which reside the soul, spirit and Divine Attributes, only this lowest and densest body is in any way organized to be manipulated by his will. The reason for this is hinted at in the story of the Fall from Eden, where Adam and Eve misused their gift of choice and were sent down into Asiyyah to be placed under the constraint of denser physical laws, where they could do the least damage until they were mature enough to re-enter Eden. Let us then begin our study of magic and miracles by examining the Asiyyatic parallel.

As has been noted, the mass of humanity works under natural law, and thus, while free will operates, it is confined to entirely physical matters. For example, mankind may profoundly interfere with the ecology of the planet, which is something no other Earth species can do. Indeed, our present pollution problems and nuclear war-games illustrate the power of modern science, which is in principle a kind of Asiyyatic magic. On the more individual level, a person may tamper with his own body and produce remarkable effects normally unknown to natural man. This is also a kind of magic, if one regards magic as a working knowledge of a particular world. The key difference between pure science and magic is will, and this belongs to the psyche and the Yeziratic World.

When dealt with intelligently, the body works well and at a high pitch over a long period. This kind of performance is possible when the laws of the body are understood and its powers developed under Will. With skilful and thorough training, the body can not only out-run a horse over a great distance but carve the most delicate filigree, handle great machines and survive in places where no animal or plant could bear to live. All this is accomplished if there is the Knowledge and Will. The same principle applies to the powers of the psychological body of Yezirah, except that in most people the organization of the psyche is not only vague and inefficient, but usually out of trim because of misuse in the current life and probably in previous lives. This situation usually precludes any manipulative skill in, let alone consciousness of, the magical World of Yezirah. The same situation occurs in the miraculous realm of Beriah, for, while the Spirit is undoubtedly present, it has no real organization beyond a general interaction of the Beriatic Sefirot. As for the Divine realm of Azilut, this remains as a remote presence, a hidden light behind a fuzzy soul and an inexperienced spirit.

In order to practise magic or perform miracles, a human being has to develop a separate and effective organism in each World, which the Will can train and then control, before acquiring the powers of those Worlds. However, besides the obvious work that has to be put in to gain the knowledge, substance and power of invisible realms, there is the question of morality.

'A man may be strong but he may not be good', runs an old proverb. In this is contained the battle between the good and evil impulse. On the physical level, natural law takes care of justice as General Providence balances things up. Thus, nations and individuals who become excessively aggressive generate opponents who check them. Likewise, when a person or nation becomes lazy, the crises created by economic poverty or political injustice stimulate work or revolution and reform. However, on the psychological level things are more subtle, and a person may think he can abuse the laws of Yezirah and escape the consequences because they cannot be seen physically. This of course is a mistake; here too the debit and credit will manifest sooner or later in life or after death. On the ordinary level of mankind this process takes care of itself, but in the case of those who have developed Will and, with knowledge, power in the invisible Worlds, the situation is different, for they can bring about effects that vegetable and animal people have no notion of. An example of this was a certain enigmatic magician of the Western tradition who could fascinate and frighten people by his deliberate use of the laws of Yezirah upon their psyches. While these demonstrations of the subtle powers of the mind were impressive, the magician's motivation was open to question. As often happens, Providence withdrew his considerable potency and knowledge, and genuine magic turned into illusion. He died, it is recorded, a perplexed old man who had forgotten what the point of the work was. It is interesting to note that the Talmud states that no magician may enter Heaven, that is, that no person still immersed in Yezirah can pass beyond the guardian Cherubim into Beriah. Such an error or misdemeanour can cost an advanced soul an important phase of its spiritual development.

Real (as against conventional) morality begins with an individual's development, because as he rises out of the lower Face of Yezirah he acquires more power to influence not only his fellows but the Yeziratic World as a whole. This occurs as the result of either a single-minded will to master the powers of Formation or as the natural fruit of spiritual development. If it is the latter, the morality of the person is watched over by the Malkhut of Beriah in the Self, which in conjunction with the Yeziratic Gevurah and Hesed purifies the psyche through the psychological Judgement and Mercy of the Soul. If the person merely wishes to acquire power in the World of Angels he is no more than a magician.

A magician is one who understands the laws and principles of Yezirah. By developing contact with his own psychological archetypes, he can gain access and use the Forces and Forms of that World. The training is long and hard, and the will has to be subjected to a rigorous discipline, because to fail during a crucial magical operation can cost a magician his sanity. The practice of magic has been in existence since remote times all over the world, because all people are constructed on the same psychological model despite differences in race, creed or personal temperament. The archetypes of Great Mother and Father are universal as are the images of the Maiden and the Trickster, the Warrior and the Great King. They occur in alchemy and astrology, and although they may appear in crude or sophisticated guises they are the same principles that operate in the witch doctor's ritual or on the psychologist's couch. For most people, direct experience of them takes place in dreams, when the unconscious clothes their forms to reflect the mood of the day. The magician merely reverses the process and makes the archetypes or angelic powers flow through a system of forms he has made and so influence psychological, then physical events according to his Will.

There is much inaccurate superstition talked and written about magic. Most of the information that is available in our culture is the dead end of a Western esoteric tradition that took aspects of Kabbalah and adopted its principles for spiritual development. Alas, often all that is left is literally the outer form or shell, without the inner content, which people attempt to practise without any discipline or knowledge of its real purpose. A person may perform an ancient and complex ritual exactly and endlessly without any result if he does not know the purpose. However, if by chance he does evoke an archetype there is a very fair chance of his being temporarily taken over by it, as many untrained magicians have found out. The reason for this is a Yeziratic law that the World of Formation is not stable by nature, and that those who seek power in it, unless well anchored below in Asiyyah, or under the obedience of Heaven in Beriah, will be swept along by the psychological tide of their own making. The ancient story of the sorcerer's apprentice who lost control of his spell, and Doctor Faustus's end in demonic disintegration, are clear warnings of the cost of practising magic without knowledge or for the wrong reasons.

In Jewish Kabbalah, magic is discouraged, although an acquaintance with its principles is expected. Needless to say, there have been Kabbalistic magicians, and their reputation down the ages bears out the efficacy of their skill. However, it must be repeated that to be caught in Yezirah in the process of spiritual growth is a great temptation, and it is an important initiation to be aware of the powers and not be fascinated by them. Indeed, the reason why the Talmud was so strict in its injunction that the magician will be denied entrance to Heaven was that many of the Jews of the post-Temple period were as preoccupied with magic as their Gentile neighbours. Such was the interest in the arts of Yezirah, that their degenerate forms continued until quite recent times, when amulets against bad childbirth or houses burning down were brought to the West by Polish and Russian Jewish immigrants in the last century.

That supernatural powers were credited to Kabbalists goes back into early history. Besides Aaron with his rod that turned into a snake before Pharaoh's magicians, there have been the various masters of what came to be called practical Kabbalah. The list of its practitioners ranges from users of the primitive sorcery of love potions and protections against the evil eye, through Rabbi Low of seventeenth-century Prague, who made a *golem* or living creature of clay, to the Baal Shem Tov, the great Wonderworker of the eighteenth-century Hasidim. Not all the accounts of the magical and miraculous events are reliable, as people often credit Wonderworkers with powers they do not actually possess, because they either wish to believe them to be real or, more probably, just like to hear an amazing tale. An example is the story of Rabbi Naphtali Cohen of Frankfurt, who was reputed to have made the sun shine at night. This was probably a total misconstruction of a psychological event in a suddenly illuminated student's mind that was reported as a literal happening. By the time the story got to the market place, the Rabbi's reputation as a magician was made, and he was subsequently accused of starting the great fire that burnt out the Frankfurt ghetto in 1711 with his practical Kabbalah experiments. Whether this particular event is true or not is irrelevant; the fact of the matter is that it is theoretically possible, if the Kabbalist has developed the ability to enter the World of Yezirah and go higher into Beriah, from where he can create the conditions that will eventually manifest in Asiyyah.

At this point it is as well to define the Kabbalistic attitude to the practical use of its knowledge. While magic is forbidden, miracles are not. Magic belongs purely to Yezirah, while miracles are the province of Beriah. Generally speaking, magic is used for individual purposes, and miracles for meeting a public need or to achieve a cosmic aim. Thus, it was permitted to ask the local Kabbalists in old Russia to create rain after all other methods had failed, or in time of national disaster to ask the aid of the Archangels who watch over the nation. The methods by which the miracles were generated were never revealed, not because they were secret but because it required a high level of being and purity to be able to enter Beriah and request the help of Azilut. The consent of God was absolutely necessary, because the balance of the whole Universe might be unduly upset by the miracles. For example, we are told in one legend that God said to a poor rabbi, 'Should I shift the balance of the World so that you can be rich? You have enough for the purpose of your life.' So in every practical Kabbalistic operation it is the Will of God that is asked for and accepted, be it for the success or failure of the enterprise. This to the practical Kabbalist is the fail-safe clause that takes away the temptation of magic for personal aggrandizement and power. Indeed, the rule is that there must be no element of gain in any sense. The operation can work only if it manifests the Glory of God.

As an example of how miracles work Kabbalistically, let us take the act of faith healing so that we may see how it operates throughout the Worlds. A man with a diseased leg comes to a Master and asks if it might be healed. The Baal Shem (which means 'Master of the Name') may or may not be a Kabbalist. If he is not, then he has been granted the gift of unconsciously being a channel to the upper Worlds. If he is a Kabbalist, and he agrees to help, he will proceed according to Sefirotic law. First, he will raise his own level up from the physical contact of his hands on the diseased limb, through to the psychological World of Yezirah, where he will imagine the form of a healthy leg. Then he will proceed higher into the Tiferet of Beriah, where he will contact, through the Keter of Yezirah, the Malkhut of Azilut. There, in the place of the God Name ADONAI, he will call upon the LORD. Here it is important to note that the miracle is not precipitated by the correct sound of the Name, as many think, but through the Kavanah or conscious intention of the Kabbalist. This is to say that the Kabbalist enters into the World of the Divine Attributes and petitions the ELOHIM for help in the matter concerned. If it is the Will of God and it concurs with the purpose of Heaven, a healthy limb is created in Beriah which then fills out the form already made by the Kabbalist in Yezirah. This then passes down via the Beriatic Malkhut of the Kabbalist into the simultaneous Tiferet or Self of the patient, and on into the simultaneous Keter of the Asiyyatic Tree of the patient's body. Here, the leg that has been Called forth, Created and Formed is remade into a healthy limb.

The above description is Kabbalistic theory, but recurring evidence reveals that the phenomenon is real. An interesting rider is that after a time the malady often returns, which suggests that either the patient cannot hold a faith link with Beriah, which is vital in order to maintain the form and substance, and so reverts to the old psychological and physical habits that created the illness, or the demonstration of the miracle has served its purpose and the Universe moves back into its original balance, while the patient, having seen what can be done by the World of Spirit, determines to do it through his own effort. This concurs with the law that while Grace is initially given to demonstrate or give a glimpse of the upper Worlds, only that won by individual merit is ever sustained. Merit is the upward evolutionary impulse, and relates directly to the level of the Kabbalist's being on the ten rungs of Jacob's Ladder.

The highest form of practical Kabbalah is that which serves the cosmic aim of bringing all the Universe into full consciousness of itself. This is traditionally called the Work of Creation, and is the reason for mankind being born into the Great Exile of the flesh. Here on Earth, Adam and Eve work to redeem not only themselves but all the Worlds of separation that seek to reunite with the Divine One of Unity.

26. Work of Unification

With the first instant of Creation at the Keter of Beriah comes separation from the Divine, and with it evil. Now evil is not, as has been said, quite the way it is generally understood. There are several kinds of evil. First, there are the demonic Forces and Forms to the extreme right and left of the three lower Worlds, and there are the Kellipot of Shells and Pit that act as the cesspool and melting pot of Forces, Forms and Consciousnesses that are in the process of being dissolved for recycling or held out of circulation until they are redeemed. These are all more or less mechanical elements in the Universal Scheme that serve a purpose as the negating and testing factors in the general evolution. Secondly, however, there is another type of evil that is particularly dangerous to mankind, and this comprises the well-organized units of free will that strive against the Common Good of Creation and indeed appear to oppose the Will of God. This kind of conscious evil works within the framework of Creation, but is separate from it in that it seeks to recreate Creation in its own image. Fortunately, by its very self-imposed isolation from the general flow, it can never gain a great or lasting hold upon events, but it can have a considerable effect because often this kind of evil is backed by considerable knowledge and knows exactly when to insert the wedge of dissension or ignorance between normally well-related sections of the cosmic community.

The source of this second kind of evil is the fact that in the process of separation from the Divine World there comes to be less and less direct influence from Azilut; this makes for deviation.

In the case of the angelic beings, the situation is safeguarded in that they not only have no individual will but are under the strict law of their function. The same is true all the way down through the Worlds, in that almost every creature is confined and fixed within the laws of its station. This also applies to the demonic hordes, which can assault but never maintain a permanent ascendancy, because by the law of their nature they destroy the very order they have invaded and revert to imbalance again. The situation for mankind is different, because of the very element of free will.

When Adam and Eve went against the commandment not to eat of the Tree of Knowledge it was not in ignorance of the Law despite their blaming of the serpent. They knew what they were doing, and in obtaining the Knowledge of Good and Evil they upset the whole balance of the Created Universe. With this act of free will, conscious evil came into being, and this is called Sin. Now the Hebrew root of the word for sin is *khata* or 'to miss the way or mark'. Here the deviation from the target is deliberate. This is possible only by an act of free will. Free will in the circumstances of Eden was not unlimited, but it was considerably greater than that which is enjoyed by mankind at present, be it living, dead or existing in Heaven or Hell. Such was the enormity of that first sin and its potential example to all other creatures, that Adam and Eve were banished from the Garden of Paradise and placed under the stricter laws of the physical realm. However, the effects are still with us and have to be corrected by Adam and Eve at every level of the Created Worlds.

The myth of this first conscious deviation has been recast in many forms down the ages. The last major Kabbalistic version was by Isaac Luria, who lived in sixteenth-century Palestine. He and his followers developed the metaphysical picture of a fracturing of the vessels of the Sefirot of Azilut below the supernal triad of Keter, Hokhmah and Binah. This, in their terms, led to a slipping down within the ladder of Worlds, so that everything was one level below its correct place. While the complex developments of the Lurianic system differ in detail from the scheme used in this book, the common principle that something is 'off the mark' is shared. So too is the idea that an individual can aid the redemption of the Worlds by his conduct and by a knowing contribution towards harmony. In this way, the conscious evil that was let loose in Creation, and is seen in the self-centred will of individuals and nations, is slowly curtailed and converted into self-control, then into the voluntary choice to submit to the Will of Heaven, which supervises the good for all despite its – to most of us – strange ways of going about it. Here one must repeat the Divine saying: 'My thoughts are not your thoughts, nor are My ways your ways' (Isaiah 55:8). While God knows everything that will happen, God will not interfere because this would take away the gift of choice. Such a view leads to the notion that evil was foreseen and indeed created to serve a cosmic purpose.

The opposition of Good and Evil is vital in the performance of free will. If there were no evil there would be no choice. Moreover, if there were no temptation to go against God, and no resistance to temptation, then there would be no application of the Will to mankind. So here we have a being which can do what it likes, within a given situation, in relation to a set of Divine Commandments. These have as their purpose not only to develop and exercise free will under a useful guideline, but to aid the Universe back into its original equilibrium before the Fall. This is why commandments have been given out by great teachers down the ages, and why apparently good people exist and participate in the midst of great suffering, if only as an example to those practising evil and as an encouragement to those who are neither particularly good nor particularly bad.

The description of the World just before the Flood is a fair picture of the incarnate human condition at its worst. From this time on, because Noah had proved man could be righteous, the human race was promised to be given a chance to sort itself out and relate to the Universe as a whole, instead of only to itself and to each individual's private interest. This still applies today, although periodically the balance of evil is so great that catastrophes like the last two World Wars occur, in order to show how far off the mark a generation is. If the present generation is perceived as the same group of souls recurring through time, it will be seen that judgement is simply being applied over a series of trans-migrations instead of over one life. As the Bible says, 'the sins of the fathers shall be visited unto the third and fourth generation', that is, the effect of one major deed will be manifested in at least three incarnations. Here it is important to add that there is the escape clause of Redemption.

Teshuvah, or Redemption, in Hebrew means to 'return to' or to 'convert'. That is, to begin to rise up Jacob's Ladder again, and not only to convert oneself into a higher state but to raise the level of everything about one. The achievement of this is either by conscious work up the central column of Knowledge, or through circumstances precipitated by the side columns of function. In the latter are the ways of Love and Fear. The Way of Love is that of the good man or woman who moves through life always aiming at the greater, which is the nature of the side of Mercy. Such people grow over many lives and even become Tsadikim or saints. They are found all over the world. There are, however, those who live by the other side column of Fear, and these comprise the vast majority of living humanity, who are not only frightened that they may starve, but often live more in dread of what the neighbours think than of how God might regard them. Fear, be it social, political or economic, rules the actions of the majority. This can create an extreme atmosphere of fear like that felt in Prohibition Chicago and Stalinist Moscow. Fear, indeed, has been a constant companion of mankind since we came out of the forests.

The result of fear is conflict, misunderstanding and suffering. If love were the dominant factor in mankind then there would be no social unrest or war. As it is, the focus is generally in the lower Face of Yeziratic Judgement, because people tend to use their free will to act from ego interest, that is against the upper Face of Yeziratic Mercy. Here is the personal contribution to the evil in the world: the denial of the true Self of the Yeziratic Tiferet. The result is suffering.

Suffering is the counterbalance to conscious evil as well as its result. It is the stern teacher that instructs that certain things should not be tolerated or continued. Thus, on a practical level, a train crash makes for an improvement in safety methods and the death of a trainload of people is not in vain for the millions of travellers who will follow in greater security. From a subtler point of view, if there were no suffering natural people would not look behind the face of phsyical life. The loss of a fortune or a dear one shocks the vegetable or animal person out of the semi-hypnotized pre-occupation with mundane events into a heightened consciousness that there is more to existence than he or she wishes to think about – even if this takes the form of angry puzzlement.

Here is where the people of the central column of Knowledge help in the performing of their cosmic function. Born into every generation and scattered throughout the world are those who are incarnated for a special purpose. While the mass of humanity slowly raises the level of the planet from the side pillars, those people called in Kabbala the Mehazdie Makla, those who reap the field, act as the direct link between the upper and lower Worlds. Their task is to teach and aid any natural person to contact his own central column and rise up to the Tiferet of his Self, so that he too can act as a link between Earth and Heaven. Such people are usually only recognized by those who are seeking something more to life, although there have been many people who, by their example, have become important public figures in the destiny of the human race. Buddha and Muhammad were obviously such men. By their lives and teaching, millions of natural men and women have sensed and even experienced the upper Worlds, and so have been able to contribute to the work of redeeming not only themselves but all Creation.

Avodah is the Hebrew word for both work and worship. Indeed, in the ancient concept, there was no difference, for every act had to be performed in honour and recollection of God. One of the reasons for the many laws in Judaism about the use of domestic utensils, for example, was to remind the householder that he must remember God, and that God gives and takes at the correct time and season. This same principle was applied in the Christian monastery. The purpose, however, is not only to recall the Deity, but to act as a vehicle for the Divine influx that flows down through the Worlds. If an individual is focused in the Self, he can transmit the flow from the Malkhut of Beriah through the

Tiferet of Yezirah and into the Keter of Asiyyah. Such action, as many great teachers have said, was needed more in the midst of evil than among the good. This is Avodah, one part of what was called the 'Work of Unification'.

The lifting of the Divine sparks that are buried in the lower depths of Creation is the occupation of mankind at large in relation to the physical World, and this it fulfils by the refining and improvement of the mineral, vegetable and animal kingdoms, despite its mistakes (which it is currently correcting, for example with anti-pollution measures and the movement for more humane and intelligent methods of farming). There are some who are concerned with aiding the redemption of those Divine sparks that are buried in the depths of lower humanity itself. Such people are usually sent down from the upper Worlds for just that mission.

The prime quality of these souls is that they know why they were born into the flesh. They may not remember it until they are mature, for like most mortals they often forget their task initially as they pass through all the normal early stages of earthly growth. However, from time to time they recall that there is something they must do, although this is not apparent in some cases until quite late in life. Usually a crisis precipitates the realization of the mission, and they perform it with all the earthly knowledge they have acquired, plus the knowledge that is inherent, and that which is imparted to them from above. This realization is sometimes called a vocation: the term, meaning 'calling', is very precise. They then go on to complete the work in the sector which has just reached the moment when someone like themselves is needed. Thus, for example, various Christian and Jewish Tsadikim or saints were born at a certain time in order that they might be present in the concentration camps of the Second World War. The effect of these people, who faced inhumanity with dignity and serenity, was enormous, both on the tormentors and on the victims. Outwardly, nothing may have appeared to have made much difference, but inwardly many died with a knowledge that death was not the end; and, among the perverse or weak people involved in running the camps, how many subsequently underwent some sort of remorse or conversion, at least a return to common decency, we shall never know. The mass result was that the German people are now extremely watchful against evil in their national life.

On a larger scale, perhaps the best-known mission of this order was that of Joshua ben Miriam of Nazareth. Born into a particularly crucial time in human history, he acted out a blameless life as an example to natural mankind of how to conduct oneself even under the most unjust conditions of physical duress, and of how to survive death. Whether he saved the world or not is a matter of Christian doctrine, but from the standpoint of Destiny he was a man trained in the traditional esoteric manner of the time, whose work brought about a major spiritual impulse in humanity. From a Kabbalistic point of view, he was one of several Benai ELOHIM or Sons of God, who have been sent down from time to time from the World of Pure Spirits to incarnate in the flesh so as to tilt the balance of the Asiyyatic World at a crucial point in history. As the result of his life and consciously given death, the spiritual level of Western civilization was raised, and a Hesedic light of love preserved; while the corrupt Roman Empire fell under another cosmic impulse, that of the invading waves of barbarians who acted as the Gevuric scourge. Out of the decadent Roman State the Church grew and maintained its spiritual link with Heaven until it, too, like all worldly organizations, became over-formalized and preoccupied with temporal power. Periodically, people like St Francis were incarnated, as was the Jewish saint the Baal Shem Tov, to remind the establishments of their duties. Unfortunately, these spiritual examples were invariably rejected by the high priests both of Christianity and Judaism. The same thing had occurred in the remote past in the East, where the Teaching had been restated in the remarkable lives of Krishna and Zoroaster, who set out to instruct many generations in the true situation of mankind and show how it could aid Creation in its evolution towards harmony with the Divine. Thus, throughout the history of mankind the Teaching has been presented again and again, each formulation adapted to the needs of the time.

The Work of Unification still continues to this day, but we must be aware that humanity's total history is but a second in a vast day that is marked out by the movement of the sun round the Milky Way, and the Galaxy's rotational year in relation to the life of the Universe. Indeed, it is said that each such solar revolution is but a Sefirotic reflection of the stage that Creation has reached as it unfolds down and then refolds up the Great Tree of Existence. In time, this vast progression must return to its penultimate state, just before the cosmic cycle moves out of Time into the Unchanging World of the Divine Azilut. The moment immediately before all Creation is dissolved is called in Kabbalah the End of Days, and towards it everything created moves in pursuit of perfection.

27. End of Days

The beginning of Existence comes into being with the Crown of Crowns, the Azilutic Keter of EHYEH – I AM. Out of the Endless Changeless World of Emanation, Creation emerges at the Tiferet of Azilut, which becomes the Keter of Beriah. From this place, the CREATOR generates the impulse of a Shemittah or Great Cosmic Cycle with all its created Worlds and creatures that inhabit them. The Sefirah of the Beriatic Keter is the second Sefirah of the Great vertical line of Light, or Will, that descends down through the central column of all four Worlds from the Keter of I AM to the Malkhut of Asiyyah in the pillow stone of Shetiyah, meaning 'Founded of God', at the very foot of Jacob's Ladder. Here is the Beginning and End of Time.

Changing Time comes into being at the Keter of Beriah. Above is the Abyss that acts as a veil between Creation and the Divine Crown of All that HAS BEEN, IS and WILL BE in existence. With change, the Great Cosmic Cycle begins to descend in a spiral that follows the Lightning Flash, that passes from right to left pillars and back again as it brings each World into being. Running through the midst of this is the unfolding central column, which is ever-present at every level of Existence. This is the Eternal Now, the presence of the Unchanging in every World that balances and reconciles the past of the left pillar and the future of the right pillar as Existence continually shifts from potential to actual, or Force to Form, and back again.

When all the Worlds were completed, the cosmic Shemittah turned at the Malkhut at the foot of Jacob's Ladder and began its retreat from the densest of materiality and complexity of law.

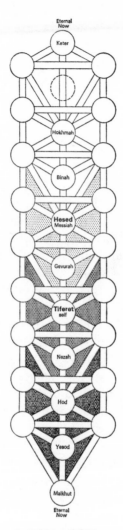

Figure 22. End of Days. *As Creation unfolds its great cycle, so Time emerges out of Eternity. The Force of the Future may crystallize into the Form of the Past, but the Eternal* NOW *is always present on the central column as the extended Line of Light draws the Sefirotic stages of Manifest Existence up into the Last Day of the Jubilee. Above the Self, at the upper place where three Worlds meet, is thest Messiah, the Anointed One, who descends just before the End of Days in order that even the spiritually dead may be raised.*

This is the evolutionary return and rising of Existence back to its source. So far in the current cycle the outgoing impulse has been accomplished with the aid of the Shekhinah or Divine Presence exiled, as it is called in Kabbalah, in the most compressed of matter. At the present time the return, if it is to be judged by the general state of mankind, is to be seen somewhere between the central nervous system and the Self, or between the Hod and Tiferet of the Great Line of Light on the central column. This places most of incarnate humanity at the level of the ego, with some above and some below.

As we have seen, the reason for the process of human incarnation is that mankind should act as a bridge between the upper and lower Worlds. In this way, the Divine Presence may be realized consciously, even in the lowest depths of physical reality, as mankind raises, for example, the metal and mineral kingdoms into the upper levels of the Asiyyatic Tree and imbues them with an intelligence they would never have experienced while buried and in an unrefined state in the earth. This is also true of the plant and animal kingdoms, whose stock, despite periodic error, is slowly being improved and protected against disease. Thus, the planet is gradually lifted in its state of awareness as mankind husbands its surface and resources.

As regards mankind itself, there are very special circumstances. Because of the gift of free will, the evolutionary process within the returning tide of the Shemittah is not automatic. People may choose to remain in the general stream of evolution, go ahead of it by individual effort on spiritual work, or even go against the cosmic flow and sink below the level of the beasts and plants into a human mineral Hell of psychological crystallization where they are fixed until Time is finished at the End of Days.

Tradition tells us that humanity is divided, according to the decisions of each individual soul, into three types corresponding to the three pillars. Those who deny that there is a purpose to existence may be said to be of the left-hand pillar, where they incur negative debts and live out life after life of severe existence. Those who go with the gradual growth of evolution are said to be of the right-hand pillar, and these people, it is said, live through generation after generation of ever-expanding circumstance. Seen as the Ways of Fear and Love, such side-pillar paths are bound by the functional laws of Force and Form. Thus, while an individual may be good or bad, he is held at that level of existence by his Karma, to use a Hindu term. In Kabbalah it is called 'Reward and Punishment until the third and fourth generation'. Thus, a person may live throughout the last part of the cosmic cycle in the incarnation of fate with its confines of pleasure or pain. The escape from this position is via the central pillar of Knowledge and Holiness.

Holiness means to be whole, that is balanced and complete, and this is the goal of those who go by the way of the central column. This Holy or Royal Way, like the other two, is also a matter of choice, except that in this case it is deliberate and conscious, as against a general and temperamental inclination towards a good or evil life. The Way of Knowledge is exactly what it says. It is sought by those who wish to know the true nature of themselves and the purpose of the Universe, and to know God face to face. In some cases such knowledge is given in one lifetime, but for most it is acquired over many lives that run parallel to the generations of the side columns. Sometimes there is a loss of the thread, and so perhaps a period of several transmigrations are spent on the left or the right pillars until the original aim is remembered. The story of the prodigal son illustrates the phenomenon well, as do many fairy tales that speak of lost miraculous objects, or people in captivity or sleep. These stories, treasured over many generations as containing more than just childish fantasy, have been written and scattered throughout the nations of the world by those belonging to the inner House of Humanity, who are responsible for helping those who wish to tread the Way of Knowledge.

The esoteric, mesoteric and exoteric levels of spiritually evolved mankind are the result of conscious work by human beings who were first incarnated perhaps very near the beginning of the time when the first Adam and Eve were born into the flesh. Some members of this upper part of the human race may be, as some traditions call them, 'old souls' – that is, they may have lived many times before on the Earth. Kabbalists have sometimes referred to them as the 600,000 original souls that were present at Mount Sinai when the Ten Commandments were given. Other traditions see them as members of ancient and lost civilizations who periodically incarnate to teach the latter-day seekers after truth. The fact that most esoteric traditions state that there are people of the higher levels, present in both incarnate and discarnate forms, indicates that the Kabbalistic concept of the spiritual Maggid or instructor is perfectly valid. More important, from this study's point of view, is that these members of the House of Israel or spiritual beings of the World of Beriah are above the law of Yezirah or Karma, that is, they are no longer subject to the influence of the Earth or the planets, although when they incarnate they pass through a single outward fate which acts as a vehicle for their long-term destiny.

We now have a picture of humanity progressing through Time, with the three living generations on the crest of the ever-present moment Now, with the past crystallizing behind into Form and the future ever opening into possibility and the potential of Force. In the midst of this returning Time are those who know the purpose of the whole operation and aid in the Work of Unification. This is done either by being in amongst the living, who are continually being reborn into situations of their own choosing, or by assisting from above in the discarnate state. Such an operation may be performed via the vehicle of the Collective Unconscious of humanity at large, or through the direct guidance of individual revelation, for a person who wishes to ascend by the central column and so gain realization quickly instead of waiting until the End of Days.

At the present time, the Work of Unification is not only the gathering in from the Great Exile of those who want to enter the Promised Land of the Spirit, but the human and cosmic operation of helping Heaven to flow down into the lower Worlds at a particularly crucial period. This movement is seen behind the two World Wars, the breakdown of the old social and political order, the enormous creativity, population growth, global consciousness, conquest of space and the undoubted new interest in things spiritual among the current generation. All this cosmic movement can go negative or positive because the choice is in the hands of mankind, which can aid or mar the balance between the Worlds.

The process of Tikune, or Amendment, is one of the major tasks of evolved people. In this they have to correct, by conscious and directed will, the oscillations between the Good and Evil of the outer columns which are stimulated by the performance of natural humanity, who live in what is called the Katnut, or Lesser State of awareness. Those in the Gadlut, or Greater State, can perceive, moreover, because of their consciousness of the upper Worlds, a slow polarization occurring between evolution and regression, as the Cosmic Cycle proceeds on its return. This recurring situation is described periodically throughout the history of mankind in myth, scripture and revelation. Up to now the tension between Order and Chaos in the macrocosm as well as the microcosm has been resolved in minor crises worked through in Heaven as well as on Earth. However, as the Shimittah comes towards the close of its great cycle at the Keter of Beriah, when every human soul has been incarnated at least once, the accumulation of all the Good and Evil that ever was, and all the affirmation and denial that has been crystallized out of the myriad individual incarnations, begins to come into hard focus as the forces for disintegration openly face those of integration. In the penultimate stage, at some point in our future, this generates the apocalyptic situation of cosmic disturbance set out in the many books of prophecy about the End of the World.

Normally, it is not given to mankind to see into the future, for two reasons: first, because it would remove the act of free will; and, secondly, because, while the general and cosmic plan is pre-arranged, the individual details are not. However, occasionally an act of Grace might allow a person to see into his own future, to warn or advise him; and it has occasionally been granted to mankind that the faculty of general prophecy be given. In this phenomenon, the future of a nation or mankind at large is perceived, so that no one is in doubt as to which side of the predicted events he wishes to choose to be on. The vision of the Biblical prophets, such as Jeremiah, on the fate of ancient Israel and her neighbours, are a classical example.

Prophecy, seen Kabbalistically, is the gift of the Hokhmah of Yezirah, or Inner Intellect. This faculty is quite different from Daat or Knowledge, in that, while the prophet may be revealing hidden things, he may not actually know what he is seeing or saying. Here is the difference between the greater prophets, who knew what they knew, and the lesser, who often fell into an unconscious ecstasy when their revelation came forth. In Kabbalah, this loss of awareness is strongly discouraged. One must know what one is about.

Revelations received by knowledge and prophecy may be personal or cosmic. They may also appertain to the local time epoch, or to the End of Days. Much of the early Apocalyptic literature refers to current and near future political events, in which recognizably existing temporal empires such as Persia, Greece and Rome fall, while the opposed faithful of Israel are preserved. However, some of these symbols should be read in their cosmic context. Seen this way, the Books of Daniel, Enoch, Baruch, the Sibylline Oracles and the Revelations of St John repeat a Universal rather than a historic theme concerning the closing stages of this particular cosmic Shemittah.

The first real sign that the End of Days is approaching is seen, we are told, when the terrestrial and celestial Worlds begin to be profoundly troubled. Both in the Heavens and on the Earth there will be major disturbances that indicate that a vast change is under way. Wars and rumours of disorder will abound. It is to be a period of trial, especially for those who are committed to aiding the process of cosmic growth, as the forces of those who deny everything but their own will seek to hold back the imminent transformation of the World. This crisis is precipitated by the fact that the accumulating level of Yezirah and Beriah present in Asiyyah is about to undergo a quantum jump of Teshuvah or conversion and redeem the physical World. Such an event is heralded, tradition and revelation says, by the appearance of Elijah, who as the incarnate presence of Enoch, the Agent of the CREATOR, announces the coming of the Messiah or Anointed One. This event is preluded by the ingathering of all Exiles into Israel; that is, all those who know of the middle column are withdrawn upward from Asiyyah, via the Self, the place of Elijah, into the Malkhut of Beriah, the Kingdom of the Spirit. Then comes the phase of the intaking of those who, on recognizing that the End of the World is at hand, leave the functional roles of the side pillars and are gathered in and accepted as proselytes to the Kingdom of Heaven. The two lower Worlds, having been evacuated of the Remnant of Israel, as all seekers of God are called in Kabbalah, then become a battleground for the evil army of Gog and Magog and the forces of the Good. In this great and final war between evolution and mechanical regression, evil is defeated and the Messiah descends from the place of the Archangel Michael, at the Tiferet of Beriah, to the Tiferet of Yezirah, to act as the Saviour King for mankind. Thus, in a glimpse of fore image, we are taught concerning the End of Days.

The position of the Messiah in Kabbalah and in many other esoteric traditions is very precise. He is the perfect human being, the living ideal for all humanity. His initial position on Jacob's Ladder is at the simultaneous Malkhut of Azilut, the Tiferet of Beriah and the Keter of Yezirah. Here, where the upper three Worlds meet in the Throne of God, he presides over the inner- most part of incarnate mankind. Whoever holds this role as the Axis of the Age is the link between the Divine ELOHIM, the Holy Spirits and humanity. The Messiah, it is said, is the true Son of God and not his servant, as all the Archangels are, despite their high rank and name of Benai ELOHIM. This special relationship is because Adam or man was God's firstborn, that is, the being who was of the ELOHIM's own begetting, in the DIVINE's own likeness. Thus it is that those of mankind who have not realized that in their Self is God seeing God are given the choice of per- ceiving the purpose of human existence in the reality of the Messiah the lastborn spirit to incarnate below. While, for example, orthodox Christians say the Messiah has come, and orthodox Jews say the Messiah is yet to come, the truth of the matter is that the Messiah has been, is, and will always be present. It could be no other way, if one knows the place of the Anointed above the Self and at the Crown of all incarnate mankind, where humanity meets ADONAI at the Malkhut of Divinity.

The apocalyptic period of the open manifestation of the Messiah to all humanity is said to be temporary, despite the fact that it is a time of great peace. Further, tradition states that during this phase of harmony Time itself slows down, as the cosmic momentum approaches its Jubilee Sabbath, so that even the planetary bodies in the physical Universe appear to progress more slowly in their orbits as all the Created Worlds and beings in them come into rest and balance. For a while, perfect Justice reigns and even death is banished, as all mankind, having been lifted out of Asiyyah and being in direct contact with Beriah, becomes aware of the spiritual Teaching concerning the purpose of Creation. This Grace is given so that no one, not even the wicked, may ignore the possibility of redemption, even in the last Seven Great Days of the Cosmic Shemittah.

On the final Day of Judgement, tradition informs us, all the spiritual records that have been collected by the angelic Watchers of the Worlds are reviewed. Here, the accumulated result of all the lives of each human being is judged according to the original cast of the particular destiny that was given at the creation of their spirit. Even the dead are resurrected on this Day of Days; that is, those who were confined for aeons to the darkest and lowest Hell of Gehinnom are released from their elemental graves to be brought up before the CREATOR who sits upon the Throne of Heaven at the Keter of Beriah. From this highest place of created existence, in the midst of the ELOHIM, the Divine Mercy and Severity is given forth upon the Archangels and Angels as well as humans. Then the totality is seen to be a single event that is fused into the common purpose again, before the CREATOR sends some into the outer darkness with its gnashing teeth beyond the order of the Azilutic Sefirot, and others back into the *Olam Ha-Ba*, 'the World to come' that begins after the *Olam Hazeh*, 'This World', is dissolved. Those creatures whose work is complete, now free of their destiny, pass beyond the seventh Heaven of Arabot and rise up out of the vast sea of Creation, crying 'I AM' as they ascend through the Abyss-Daat of Azilut and into union with the Crown of Crowns, beyond which they individually merge into the knowing and being of God.

Below, at the Tiferet of Azilut, the CREATOR Wills another general Shemittah, to unfold the new Universe. In this next Sefirotic step are the seeds of everything great and small, high and low, that will happen in the following manifestation of Existence, which thus proceeds, cosmic cycle by cosmic cycle, towards the Jubilee of Jubilees. In this final and full realization of everything Called forth, Created, Formed and Made, the Immanence present will directly mirror the Transcendent. Thus, the original of all intentions will be fulfilled when all the Worlds are unified in the image of fully divine Adam so that there is no separation, as God beholds God. In this knowing and being known, we are told, the ABSOLUTE ALL is realized in the ABSOLUTE NO-THING. Then, EN SOF merges with AYIN and the Mirror. Existence vanishes leaving God the ONE. 'God's place is the World, but the World is not God's place.'

Glossary of Kabbalistic Terms

Asiyyah: World of Making.
AYIN: Absolute No-thing.
Azilut: World of Emanation. Divine Glory.
Beriah: World of Creation. Pure Spirit. Archangels.
Binah: Sefirah of Understanding and Reason.
Daat: Non-Sefirah of Knowledge. The Abyss.
Edom: Incomplete Worlds, or natural mankind.
Ego: Yesod of Yezirah – Foundation in man of psyche.
EN SOF: Absolute All, or the Infinite without End.
Gehinnom: Hell, Kellipot of the Pit.
Gevurah: Sefirah of Judgement, sometimes known as Din.
Gilgulim or Gilgul: Transmigration of souls or rebirth.
Haiot Hakodesh: Four Holy Living Creatures – Man, Eagle, Lion and
    Bull – at Keter of Yezirah.
Hasid: A pious man, a saint of Hesed.
Hesed: Sefirah of Mercy or Love.
Hod: Sefirah of Reverberation, echo or Glory.
Hokhmah: Sefirah of Wisdom and Revelation.
Israel, House of: Inner and upper level of mankind. Same as Christ's
    Church.
Jubilee: End of a Great Cosmic Cycle.
Kavanah: Prayer with conscious intention.
Kellipot or Qliphoth: World of Shells and disorder, demonic realms.
Keter: Crown of Tree of Life.
Maaseh Bereshit: Work of Creation.
Maaseh Merkabah: Work of the Chariot.
Maggidim: Spiritual Teachers.
Malkhut: Lowest Sefirah, called the Kingdom.
Menorah: Seven-branch candelabrum of Moses.

Merkabah: Chariot, or Yeziratic World of Psyche.

Messiah: The Anointed One. Axis of Age. The perfect incarnate man at Keter of Yezirah.

Metatron: Archangel of Presence at Keter of Beriah. Enoch as Spirit.

Nefesh: Natural Soul, i.e. vegetable and animal vitality.

Neshamah: In this system, the human soul. Yeziratic triad of Gevurah-Hesed-Tiferet.

Nezah: Sefirah of Eternity or Repeating.

Sandalphon: Archangel of Self at Malkhut of Beriah.

Sefirot: Lights, vessels, faces, etc., of the Ten Divine Emanations.

Shekhinah: Divine Presence in Malkhut of Azilut and below.

Shemittah: Great Year or Cosmic Cycle.

Shetiyah: Foundation Stone of the World. Jacob's Pillow.

Sitra Ahra: Evil impulse.

Sitra HaKedesha: Holy impulse.

Teshuvah: Redemption or Conversion.

Tiferet: Sefirah of Beauty at centre of Tree of Life.

Tikune: Conscious amendment to cosmic imbalances.

Yesod: Sefirah of Foundation.

Zahzahot: The Three Hidden Lights in the Godhead.

Zelem: An image.

Zimzum: The Contraction within the Godhead to allow existence to come into being.

Index